BEYOND THE
MEADOW

BEYOND THE
MEADOW

ANN B. THOMPSON

Library of Congress Control Number: 2007903379
ISBN: Hardcover   978-1-4257-5996-4
                 Softcover   978-1-4257-5980-3

To order additional copies of this book, contact:
Xlibris Corporation
1-888-795-4274
www.Xlibris.com
Orders@Xlibris.com
38737

CONTENTS

Chapter 1: The Meeting on the Plane 11

Chapter 2   Elizabeth and Dan in the Meadow 19

Chapter 3   Elizabeth Goes Looking for Her Past 26

Chapter 4   Making Plans for the Research 32

Chapter 5   Following Leads 38

Chapter 6   Her Own Hometown 46

Chapter 7   Father Located 54

Chapter 8   Mother Located 60

Chapter 9   Elizabeth Meets Her Sister 66

Chapter 10 A Sister's Gift 72

Chapter 11 The Trunk: Elizabeth Discovers the Truth 79

Chapter 12 The Journals 85

Chapter 13 Closure for Dan 96

Chapter 14 The Final Chapter 102

Dedication

To my wonderful sister-in-law, Ellen, who read with patience and endurance my first book and encouraged me to continue on, and to my family, my two daughters and my husband, who continue to believe in me, I can never express how grateful I am to each of you for such loyalty.

Love is the river of life in this world. Think not that ye know it who stand at the little tinkling rill—the first small fountain. Not until you have gone through the rocky gorges, and not lost the stream; not until you have gone through the meadow, and the stream has widened and deepened until fleets could ride on its bosom; not until beyond the meadow you have come to the unfathomable ocean, and poured your treasures into its depths—not until then can you know what love is.

—Henry Ward Beecher

CHAPTER 1

The Meeting on the Plane

Nothing in life just happens. Each single thread of our very fiber is interwoven with every other thread. There is always a reason behind every path we take and every road we travel. Even though we stumble blindly along life's road, we are never without guidance or goals. It is often in the afterglow that we realize our goals were met because of an unpredicted turn we made or an unexpected path we traveled. That, in a few short sentences, had always been Elizabeth's hypothesis for living life. When her life would become a jumble, seemingly swirling out of control, she was always sure there had to be a reason; and someday, hopefully, she would realize what that reason was. If not, then she would feel that she just couldn't see the reason and would simply move on. When things were going good, she felt the same way. Thus, she had always gone through life one day at a time, accepting the bad with the good and living it moment by moment.

She had recently become a successful writer. That was one turn, in her chain of events, she had never expected. Something had prompted her to write a book about two people separated by time, who managed to find each other in a lovely meadow. There was no hot sex, no grossly descriptive murder. She thought it was just a pleasant book to read with a happy ending. Many people must have thought so as well, for she was now on the best-seller list. She had never really ever expected to become an author, much less a best-selling author. That was something she was totally unprepared for. Her life had become a jumble of travel and hurry, of appointments and interviews. She had been invited to do book signings in many different places, and she was on her way home from one of those now. This was it for Elizabeth! She had had enough travel to last the rest of her life. She really disliked travel, especially air travel, and she was ready to hideaway now and catch up on her artwork.

She boarded the plane as soon as she could. Normally she didn't fly first class, but her ticket had somehow gotten upgraded, and she was quite pleased with that. She was going to publish a barn calendar for next year, with a different one of her barn drawings for each month. She was in the process of trying to finish up the last two of them now. Five hours on the plane should see the completion of at least one of them, and being able to sit in first class would give her the room to spread out and work. The latest barn was her favorite. She had found it just off the interstate north of Charlotte. The pictures she had gotten of were good ones even though she had not been able to get up very close.

She let her seat slightly backward and rested her head on her pillow. She wanted to relax just a few minutes before she started the drawing. Her mind wandered back to the book she had written and how she came to write it. If you had asked her five years ago or even a year ago about writing a book, she would have laughed at the thought she might even consider doing that. At no time in her life did she ever have aspirations of being a writer. She never liked to write and had never even written a short story. Truth be known, Elizabeth was never much of a reader either. The love she had for reading in her youth gave way to housework, children, and art. She always seemed to have other things she preferred to do. She loved sewing, crafts making, and anything that involved working with her hands. Reading didn't allow for interruptions, and her life had been one continual interruption, so she had simply stopped.

One day, a story had come to her. The whole thing just seemed to be there suddenly in her mind, from who knew where, and she felt the urge to write it down. It was an interesting-enough plot involving two people from different centuries. She had woven in parts of her life with parts of the story. The meadow she had described was actually hers. It was exactly as the story had told, created in her mind as part of a meditation exercise. The muscle disorder was hers as well. She had moved to Charlotte to be closer to her daughter, and she did love to draw. Those were all actually part of Elizabeth's life. The rest of the story just came to her in pieces and parts. She remembered the nights she would wake up with conversation in her head that belonged in the story or people or ideas that seemed to all go together. It seemed that almost every night, from the day she started the book until it was finally done, she would wake up sometime around three thirty or four in the morning with new ideas for the story. She had kept a tape recorder by her bed finally so that she could just record the thoughts that were there. She remembered drawing the face of Dan, the main character, with no idea how he would look and with not much ability to draw faces. The whole story thing had taken over her life, and somehow she seemed driven to finish the novel. "Driven" was the word her daughter had used, but she felt more like it had been an obsession. She didn't seem to really have any control over the story at all. She simply wrote down what she would wake up knowing. A few of the facts were hers, but the rest was more like some type of inspiration.

What had started out to be maybe a yearlong project gave her no rest until she had finished, and it took only three months. She was very glad to have it done. Now, she was sleeping at night again, and life seemed to be back on track. She had gone back to her artwork, but her daughters had liked her book very much and urged her to publish it. The next thing she knew, it was on the market and selling well.

She had published under a pen name with no picture on her book. Publicity was not something she was anxious to have. She had no intentions of making writing a new career at this stage in her life. She was just glad to have gotten this book out of her system. The pen name was an excellent idea as well. Her publisher had forwarded her all the mails she received. It was amazing how many Dan Kerrs had written her to claim they were "the one" or a relative of the one in her book. Many others had claimed the meadow and offered to let her come and take pictures; even some wrote in claiming to be Amy. Elizabeth was overwhelmed by how much mail came in to the company for her. She had never responded to any of them, and eventually she grew tired of even reading them.

For now, it was five hours of peace and quiet. Hopefully the trip home would be uneventful, and she could get some work done. She would just rest her eyes a few more minutes and then finish the barn. Elizabeth drifted off in peaceful sleep.

Waiting in airports was just about Dan's least favorite thing in the whole world to do, but he had spent many hours doing exactly that. He was a successful real estate promoter and builder. His base office was in Detroit; but twenty years ago, he had purchased a large track of farmland just north of Charlotte, North Carolina. He had opened another office there, and now he spent a great deal of his time these days flying back and forth between the two. He had an hour to kill today before the plane was ready to take off, so he wandered off to find something to eat.

Airport food never held much appeal for him either, so he just ordered coffee and sat thinking. For some reason today, his mind wandered back to that land he had purchased and what he had found there. It seemed like a lifetime ago now, but still the images from that summer remained fixed in his heart as though it had just happened.

Just about smack-dab in the middle of that track of land had been a meadow. It was unusually green and well kept with a brook that flowed along beside it. He remembered the first time he found that spot. He had bought the farm, sight unseen. A friend of his had called and suggested it might be something he should consider. It had great potential and was in an excellent location. A shopping mall and some large subdivisions were what he had planned to put in there. He had flown down to look over the property for himself and in doing so had stumbled on this beautiful place. Walking through the property, he found an open meadow with a stream and a large shade tree. He had felt an immediate sense of peace come over him there. What a welcome change that had been from his usually hustle-and-bustle life. There was a very interesting thing about that meadow. While the rest of the farm was overgrown with weeds or planted in crops, this area remained well tended and free from any crop. It looked as though someone continued to tend it even though the property had been on the market for over a year.

He sat down there in that field, leaning against the old oak tree, and was watching the brook go by when he saw a woman walking across the meadow alone. She was wearing what looked like a nightgown of sorts, carrying a wide-brimmed hat, and she was barefooted. He was not aware of anyone living anywhere close to the property, and it was a very large piece of land he had bought. She saw him; their eyes locked. He looked around to see where she had come from, but when he looked back, she was gone.

He had not planned to stay in Charlotte for long, only long enough to look over the property and then turn the project over to someone there; but before the summer was over, he had not only stayed there but established an office, fallen deeply in love, and the property had proven to be more profitable than he ever imagined. His life had been turned upside down that summer, and his world had never been the same again.

Sitting in the airport restaurant, he could still remember the tingling undertow of emotion he felt that summer when he first saw Emily. It was a strange sensation, almost, he thought—like how one would feel if they woke up not knowing where they were yet feeling like they must have arrived in some safe haven. He felt like he had been misplaced, but he was supposed to be. There really was no way to describe how he felt, but it was the same tingle he had felt when he stopped in a little gift shop in the airport to buy a book to read on the airplane some six months ago. He noticed a small novel there in the stands that took his breath away. There in the new release rack was a small book. *The Meadow* was the title, and the picture on the front of the book was none other than his meadow. It was beyond explanation, but there it was. The author had apparently written under a pen name, and, try as he might, for the last three months he had been unable to locate her.

He desperately wanted to find this woman. He had contacted the publishing company numerous times trying to get in touch with her but with no success. He had located a book signing she was supposed to have attended in Detroit one weekend, but weather had cancelled her appearance. He always carried that book in his briefcase. Somehow, someway, someday, he was going to locate this author. He just had to.

Dan had never confided in anyone about what had happened to him that summer in the meadow. It was personal and private. He was unable to tell anyone. That summer had held one surprise after another for him, and he had no relative or friend to whom he would have revealed those events. It had been twenty years ago now, and still he did not understand how it could have happened. Having read the book, the question now was, How could this woman have gotten so many details of that summer, written them down, and never talked to him? Yes, he must find her. He was sure she had to know the answers to all his questions.

He was the last to board the plane. He liked it that way. It was going to be a long flight, and he had plenty of work to get done. He disliked travel, but at least by plane, they did the driving, and he got to work. He always traveled first class. He was a big man and hated to be cramped into a small seat with his laptop and papers. This trip, the plane was full to capacity. The only seat left now was his.

Usually he didn't feel faint or light-headed, but suddenly he felt his knees buckle, and the blood rush to his head. He had never fainted before, but he was sure this was how it felt just before one went down. He felt his body leaning too far to the right. The attendants realized at once, he was in trouble and came immediately to his rescue.

"Are you all right, sir? You are very pale." She supported his arm and motioned to the other attendant to do the same on his other side. They helped him to his seat and brought him something to drink. Dan was regaining his composure.

"Yes, thank you, I think I am okay now. I don't know what happened there. Must have been something I ate." *Liar!* he said only to himself. He knew exactly what happened. There! Right there on the plane was a lady sitting in the seat next to him who made his knees buckle and his head reel. She looked almost exactly like he was sure an older version of someone he had loved and lost would look. He was sure that if she had lived, she would have been this woman's twin. The passenger he was sitting next to had the same stubborn jawline, the same dark hair. She seemed to be sleeping, unaware of his predicament or the fact that Dan had not taken his eyes off her since he boarded. The plane lifted off, and he sat there studying her intently. This had to be the woman who had penned the book, the woman he had been searching for. She looked like Emily; it had to be her. He didn't know what quirk of fate had put them on that plane together, side by side, but he was sure it was meant to be.

Her eyes fluttered open. She jumped slightly. Now she was aware that someone had taken the seat beside her. They had not only taken the seat, but she could feel him looking at her intently.

"Oh my." She laughed. "I must have dozed off. Was my mouth hanging open and drool running out?"

"No, why would you ask that?" He was embarrassed. He realized he had been staring at her, and she must have been aware of it.

"I guess it was the look on your face." She didn't want to stare at him, but he looked very much like the picture of the character she had drawn in her book. She wasn't about to say that since no one knew she was the one who had written the book. She didn't want to just look straight at him because she was very aware that he was more than a little interested in her, but he had the same chin and the same frown. She dismissed it as coincidence, but still it was a bit unusual for someone to resemble her character that closely since she had created him completely from her mind. To distract herself from the urge to stare back at him, she got out her barn to finish. She realized he was still watching her closely.

"You do have done a great job with that barn. I always envied people who could draw."

"Do you like barns?" She was trying to make light conversation. Somehow she was still feeling very uneasy.

"Yes, I especially like the one you are drawing."

"Thank you. I think it is my favorite. It sits just off I-85 north of Charlotte. For some strange reason, I have always been partial to this particular barn. I am making a calendar for next year of old barns, and this one is going on the front."

"Yes, I know exactly where that barn is. Would you believe me if I told you that was my barn?"

"No." She laughed. "Of course, I don't believe much of what anyone tells me lately. There is a good reason for that."

"I should introduce myself, but I think I already know who you are."

"Really? Who am I?" Elizabeth was starting to wish she had just kept sleeping. This conversation was really starting to make her uncomfortable now.

"I don't believe I know your real name, but your pen name is Ann Thompson. Am I correct?"

Bingo. No one had identified her before. Of course, she had been to many book signings now and was becoming more and more visible. That wasn't an advantage.

"Yes," she admitted with reluctance, "you caught me. The real name is Elizabeth Scott, and your name is?"

"Dan Kerr."

Oh no, Elizabeth thought to herself, *please just make him go away.* There had been several look-alikes at every book signing, and they always wanted some type of publicity. There had been two in particular who had been forcibly removed from the scene by the police. It was more than a little embarrassing. Now here was one sitting next to her on a plane. Suddenly she was wondering if he had somehow gotten her ticket upgraded to get her in this seat. "What did you want from me, Mr. Kerr?" The annoyance in her voice was obvious.

Dan saw where this was going and was quick to avoid it. "I want nothing that I can think of. I just happen to have that name. It's not my fault, honestly. My mother did give it to me." He tried to laugh and sound casual. Dan wasn't really very good at neither making idle conversation nor laughing, but he wasn't going to say anything at this point to scare her away. He had been looking for this woman for months now, and somehow fate had put them side by side on an airplane going to Charlotte. What he hadn't expected was for the author of this book to look so much like Emily. He got out his briefcase and tried to look busy. He was trying to think of a way to keep a connection with her after the plane landed when she interrupted his thoughts.

"Are you going to Charlotte?" Now she was trying to make pleasant small talk to ease the obvious tension she felt between them. She had not meant to offend him, but she was prepared to ward off any publicity-stunt advances before they got started. He looked so much like the picture she had drawn. She felt ill at ease sitting there in silence.

"Yes, I have a company office there and another one in Detroit. I seem to spend more time on planes than I do in either of them lately. When business allows, I prefer to be in Charlotte. The weather is definitely warmer there. Is that where you live?"

"Yes, I moved there several years ago, and I just love it; but I still don't know my way around very well." She liked his voice. It was deep and calming with a slight Southern drawl. Interesting, since he was from Detroit, that he would sound Southern. Feeling a little more at ease now, she was curious, and she asked him, "Is this really your barn?"

Now the frown turned to a smile. "Yes, in fact it really is. That is a nice view of it too, but I believe that from the other side, it looks even better. You really need to take the picture from the field and not the road to get the best angle."

"I didn't know how to get there. When I found it, I didn't see anywhere to turn in, so I took it from the highway. Often when I take pictures of old barns, I can find a road or at least a pull off, and I am able to drive right up to the barns and walk around them. I didn't see a place to do that with this one."

"Would you like for me to take you there sometime?" Dan was relieved she had believed him. He was definitely not after any publicity. That was the last thing he wanted. He did have something he wanted from Elizabeth, but publicity was not it.

"That would be nice, really. I could save the front cover for the other side of the barn. Would you have time on this trip to Charlotte? How long are you staying?"

What a break. This was his chance to see her again. That was much easier than he had expected. Would he have time? If he had no time, he would make time for this lady. He wasn't going to say any more about the barn. She could just see it for herself. There was a surprise waiting for Elizabeth at the barn, and now he wondered how she would feel when she discovers it. If she thought his looks and name were a publicity stunt, she would avoid him forever if he told her what lay just the other side of the barn.

"Certainly, I will take the time. I love that old barn as well and would be honored to have it on your calendar. I had planned to be here for a couple weeks, but my schedule is usually flexible. If tomorrow wouldn't be too soon, I could call you when I am free, and we will take a ride out there and have some lunch on the way. I have a nine o'clock meeting that should last a couple hours; then I'm free all afternoon." Dan handed her a business card. That was to assure her he really was Dan Kerr and he really was a businessman. Most of all, he wanted her to have his phone number. He wrote his cell phone number on the back for good measure.

"That would be very nice, thank you." Elizabeth wrote down her address and phone number for him as well. The rest of the trip was small talk or no talk. Dan got busy with

17

his work. He wanted to talk and talk to her, but he wasn't sure what he could say just now that wouldn't scare her away. He had dozens of questions to ask her, but this was neither the time nor the place for them. It took an enormous amount of self-control to keep all his thoughts and feelings inside. He had so many questions about the book and questions about how she got the story. He wanted to ask her all of them at once. Maybe once she saw the barn, he could explain it to her, and she would understand. After all, hadn't she been the one who wrote a book about just exactly what had happened to him? If anyone would understand and explain it all to him, she would. Tomorrow was going to feel like it was a lifetime away.

CHAPTER 2

Elizabeth and Dan in the Meadow

Dan called Elizabeth just after one in the afternoon.

"Sorry, I guess I am running late. I thought sure that meeting would be over before now. Did you give up on me and eat lunch already?"

"No, I wasn't in any hurry, and I understand how those meeting can run over."

"Great. I know a little café where we can grab a quick bite. I am on my way now. It should take me about fifteen minutes to get to your place. I'm not far from there now."

He was prompt and polite. Elizabeth liked that. Interesting, she didn't feel at all skeptical about riding off in a car with a total stranger. What would her daughter say? She felt unusually relaxed and safe with him. They had a quick and unusually quiet lunch at a small locally owned sandwich shop. Dan was reluctant to say anything about his mission. After lunch, they headed up the interstate toward the barn.

Dan pulled off the highway and onto a side road that looked like nothing more than a path. They seemed to be in the middle of nowhere, and Elizabeth was starting to wonder if she should have ridden here with someone she didn't really know. She had not even told her daughter where she was going or whom she was going with so no one would know what happened to her or where she had gone. He parked the car in a clearing beside the barn. Well, at least they did go to the right barn. Elizabeth let out a sigh of relief and got out to take a few more pictures.

She had several pictures of this barn already that she had taken from the highway, but it was wonderful to be able to get up close to it and study the details of the structure. She could almost hear children laughing as they jumped from the loft into a stack of hay or smell the horses as they came in for their evening meal. Barns were such wonderful things. Most of them held memories of childhood and growing up as well as families and communities growing and building together.

"You might want to take a few from back here. This angle shows the barn's best qualities," he called. His voice interrupted her thoughts and brought her back to her mission. She looked around to see where his voice had come from. He had walked some distance out in the field and was standing, waiting for her there.

"Okay, I'm on my way. I was just taking a few more from this angle while I'm here. I just love this barn. It is strange that I have such an attachment for this particular one.

I always loved them all but never felt any special connection to any of them before. I almost feel like I played in this one as a child. That's funny because I grew up in Kentucky. Not much chance of my being here."

Elizabeth walked toward Dan not thinking until she was midfield and almost touching him, how much this looked like the meadow she had created in her mind and written about in her book. Suddenly it all came crashing down. This was the meadow! There was the brook, the fence on the other side, the trees, and the big willow oak. Amy sat down suddenly; her face was pasty white. Everything was black for a minute, and then it all came back into focus.

"Are you okay?" Dan looked very concerned. The frown that seemed to be his usual expression deepened. He had expected she would be surprised, but he had not thought she would collapse.

"No, I don't think I am." So this was a publicity stunt after all. How could he create this place so accurately? Every detail was exactly as she had seen it in her mind, but not all of those details were in the pictures that she had drawn for the book. Not all the details were written in the book either. Only she would have known them all. How would he have known?

"I was sure you would recognize it when you saw it." He sat down beside her now. He knew she might bolt from the meadow if he tried to reach out and touch her, so he just sat perfectly still next to her, waiting for her to recover.

"So you knew about this, and you let me just walk in here without any warning. What did you expect to accomplish? Did you create this meadow for a publicity stunt?" By now, Elizabeth had recovered from the sudden shock of seeing the meadow firsthand and was angry. The man she had met on the plane, the man she had believed and trusted, suddenly wasn't at all who she thought he was.

Elizabeth knew that he had not created this place. Even as she was accusing him of doing so, she knew it just wasn't possible. There was just no way he could have made this wonderful place, but she preferred to hear him say that he did create all this for publicity than to think what the alternative might be.

Dan had expected she would think a lot of things, but that wasn't one he was ready for. Publicity was one thing that had not occurred to him. This place was so private to him, he wasn't sure he should have brought Elizabeth here, but he needed her help. "I'm sorry. I didn't want to scare you off, but I needed you to see this. There was no way to tell you about this. It is my meadow. It belongs to me, and I have preserved it as such for the last twenty years. I have been careful not to change anything here—not the trees or the fence line or even the flowers. I do not want publicity. That would be the last thing on earth I would want. This is a very private spot, not a place where I have ever brought anyone before. If I had told you what you would find here behind this barn, you would have never come with me. You would have been sure it was a publicity stunt or worse, and I would never have seen you again. The truth is, I needed you to be here."

"But I created this place in my mind years ago. How did you get this meadow to look exactly like the one I pictured and wrote about?" Elizabeth had heard him, but her thoughts were being verbalized even as they came to her. "What do you mean you needed me here?"

"That's the whole point, Elizabeth, I don't think you really did create this in your mind. I believe the details of this beautiful spot were given to you somehow by Emily."

"Emily who? Who is Emily anyway? How could someone I don't know pass the vision of a meadow to me? What makes you think she would pick me anyway?"

"That is the part I am not sure of, but I am sure that you are the key to me finding someone that I lost almost twenty years ago. That is why I needed you here."

Elizabeth was somewhere north of Charlotte, in the middle of an abandoned field, with a person she didn't know, who was now talking like a crazy man. It was useless to run. Where would she run to anyway? She wasn't even sure where they were. He didn't appear to be dangerous at the moment, so she might as well hear him out. Then she would get him to drive her home, say thank you, and hope he never called her again. It would be an afternoon she would laugh about years later, hopefully.

Dan tried to explain the situation as concisely as he could. "I purchased this farm twenty years ago, sight unseen as a real estate investment. The plan was to develop it into shopping malls and subdivisions. I came here just after the purchase to look over the plot. I was in my forties. I met a young woman in the same manner as you described in your book. I never told anyone about it. She lived in a different time frame, but somehow she came here to me in this meadow. Apparently her parents owned this farm some years back. Her name was Emily, and had I known her when she was your age; I am sure she would now look almost exactly like you. One day she just stopped coming to the meadow. There are a lot more details to the story as I'm sure you can imagine, but that is pretty much it in a nutshell."

Amy was still sitting in the middle of the meadow. She looked from one corner to the other. The frightening thing was this is exactly how she had pictured her meadow some twenty years ago when she had first started meditation. She had thought maybe a seashore scene with wave crashing and gulls flying, but for some reason this picture kept coming back to her. Finally, she had dismissed the seashore and settled for this beautiful place.

She had never regretted it. For years, it had been her place of refuge. She had even managed to go there during some painful surgical procedures and escaped the pain. The unfortunate part of writing her book had been the meadow. She had shared it with the world as a story but destroyed it for herself. Once she had started writing her story, the meadow was useless to her. She could go there, but once there, she spent the whole time thinking about the characters in her book and what they were doing and thinking. It had been useless, and she had sadly given up her beautiful spot as a place of escape for her. Now, she was sitting on it. The difference was now she could see the full spectrum of the meadow within the countryside. There were other meadows and fields layered up the slopes, and the majestic mountains rose above them all. It was a panoramic view that was breathtaking. The stream flowed from somewhere up the mountain and curved just at the end of the meadow. The quiet gurgling of the water, flowing along, added the last touch of serenity to the already-perfect spot. She felt the breeze gently stirring through her hair. She felt as though she had somehow gotten into a meditative state, and she had the uncontrollable urge to reach down and take off her shoes.

Dan watched her as she removed her shoes. Emily had always come to the meadow barefoot. He had to put his hands in his pocket to keep himself from reaching out and pulling Elizabeth to him. He desperately wanted to hold her. He knew she would feel exactly as Emily had felt. He was sure this was Emily who retuned to him. Twenty years of loneliness and the reappearance of Emily were almost more than Dan could deal with. Now, here he sat alone in the meadow with this woman, who was obviously somehow connected to him and Emily and the meadow. His memories of the hours there were as vivid now as if they had happened only yesterday. How could he convince Elizabeth that she was either Emily or some relative of hers? Better yet, how could he convince himself that he wasn't dreaming this whole thing?

Her voice cut through his memories: "I don't know anyone named Emily."

She wasn't looking at him any longer like he had lost his mind. She was aware of something strange in this meadow. She realized that he didn't appear as crazy as he sounded. After all, hadn't she written a story that happened exactly that way, and she didn't think it was crazy at all? Even though it was only a story, she had always been a firm believer in true love seeking its own, even across time.

"Was your grandmother named Emily? Or maybe your aunt had that name? Or even a distant cousin who might have been named Emily? There had to be someone. I am sure you are the connection that I have searched for." Dan's voice sounded desperate, and it made Elizabeth slightly uncomfortable.

"I wish I could help you, Mr. Kerr, but I was adopted as a baby. No one in my adopted family had that name; of that I am sure. I never located my birth parents. I never had a desire to do so, and I have no idea what their names were. I wouldn't know where to start."

Dan looked as if she had slapped him. He had been so sure this woman would have the answers he had looked for. He had such high expectations since he found Elizabeth; he could not imagine he would be disappointed. After years of wondering and then seeing Elizabeth on that plane, he never expected to reach a dead end so abruptly. His shoulders slumped, and Elizabeth thought he was going to cry.

"I guess I could try and look into my past if it would help you." She felt the need to say something to give him some hope. He looked so desolate and brokenhearted. It was the least she could do.

His face brightened immediately. "Would you? I mean I wouldn't want you to do this if it is going to be painful for you, but I have waited some twenty years now to find the answer to my questions. Somehow fate found you for me, and I was so sure you would just have all the answers; it is hard to accept a dead end."

"I can try. It won't be painful at all. I have a very realistic view of my past. I don't know how much success I will have though. It has, after all, been sixty-two years. Who knows what kind of trouble I will have finding them. I can't make any promises."

"I am pretty good at computer research if that will help you." Dan was anxious to continue contact on a more frequent basis with Elizabeth. He knew she wasn't Emily, but he already felt as though he knew her and wanted to see more of her. "If you could get me any kind of names or states or cities, I could do a concentrated search."

She was already starting to think what she could do and where she would start. "My brother found his birth parents after both our adoptive parents had died. I will check with him and see how he got started. That might help. He didn't seem to have much trouble finding them. I'm sure he will help me look as well."

"I know this will be hard for you, Elizabeth, but I feel like you are the key to what happened to me here in this field. The whole experience was so bizarre that I never told anyone about it until now. I am not one to believe that things just happen. I feel there has to be always a reason behind them, and I need to know the reason. I firmly believe that your book is somehow directly connected to Emily."

"I will do what I can. I always felt like the story of my book was given to me from some unknown source like I was writing someone's story. Once I had started writing, it seemed to take control of my mind until it was finished. Perhaps you are right. Maybe both of us will uncover answers we are looking for."

"If you think it was a shock for you to see this meadow, think how I must have felt when I not only saw my meadow on your book cover but read my own story that someone else had written. No one knew that story but me. I tried for months to reach you. I wrote and called everyone I knew. You are very good at avoiding publicity."

"I got so much mail forwarded to me from the company that I finally just stopped reading it. I would never have believed your letter anyway, I'm sure. You were right. I had to be here in the meadow to fully understand what is happening. I will do what I can to find answers for both of us."

Dan drove Elizabeth back to the city. They had stayed in the meadow talking and sharing thoughts and ideas for solving this mystery longer than either one had realized. Elizabeth had loved seeing her meadow and being able to not only sit in the middle of it but take dozens of pictures of it for her later artwork. It was growing dark by the time they got back to the city. "Could I take you to dinner, Elizabeth? It's the least I could do to thank you for being such a help to me. I actually know a place that isn't a fast-food spot." Dan had found her, and he was in no hurry at all to let her go.

Elizabeth was starting to like and trust Dan. By now, she realized he definitely wasn't out for publicity, and he seemed to need more answers than she did if that were possible. She was in no hurry to leave his company either. "Yes, thank you, that would be very nice if you have the time. I don't want to keep you tied up if you need to work. I know you must be very busy."

They chose a quiet Italian eatery with few customers. Elizabeth still had some questions for Dan. Over dinner, they continued going over and over the details of what Elizabeth had written as compared to what Dan had actually lived. They were strikingly similar.

"In my book, there was a strange little man with a book. I was never sure why I put him in there. I never really was sure he even fit in the story. Do you have anything like that or ever meet anyone like that?"

"No, I never met any strange man, but Emily had a little brown leather book once that had stories about people in similar situations. She said some peddler gave it to her. I never saw the book or the peddler, but she told me about it. She somehow believed the book had something to do with us meeting in the meadow or maybe meeting again later. I was never sure what it was all about."

"What happened to Emily?"

"I don't really know. I just always assumed when she didn't return to the meadow that something dreadful had happened to her. I didn't know if she died or moved away or was forced to stay away from the meadow. Whatever happened, I was sure it was bad; otherwise, she would never have left me without telling me where she was going. She always appeared to be in some type of nightgown, and even though she never mentioned anything, I felt as though somehow she was sick or dying all along. When she didn't come back, I was positive she must have died."

"Maybe she came back to the meadow after you left."

"I doubt that. I stayed on here in Charlotte up to the winter, but she never returned. I spent as much time as I thought I could around this property without raising eyebrows in the community. Eventually, I just gave up waiting and went back to Detroit."

"I am very sorry, Dan. Even as I was writing the book, I envied the characters' deep love. I think, to have known that type of love even for a short time would be worth whatever comes."

"I don't know about that part, but I never got over her, and I never married. So far, no one has ever been able to fill her place in my heart. I always go back out there when I am in town. I find peace in the meadow, and I somehow feel connected to her no matter how long it has been. I keep it maintained at all times. If she should have ever wanted to come back, it would be ready for her."

"Well, I will start first thing in the morning and see what I can find out. You have my curiosity aroused now as well. I have a few answers of my own to find. If there is an Emily in my background somewhere, we will find her if she can be found."

Dan drove Elizabeth home and walked her to her door, but he knew better than to reach for her. He was afraid that once he held her, he would not be able to let go. He desperately wanted to just draw her next to him and hang on to her forever. Instead, he leaned forward and kissed her on the cheek. Certainly, she wasn't ready for him to engulf her totally yet. He would wait. He was sure Emily must have led him to Elizabeth, and he was not disappointed. After all these years, maybe there was someone who could take Emily's place in his heart. He would wait. After all, hadn't he waited some twenty years now? What were a few more months?

"Good night, Elizabeth. Thank you for hearing me out. I will call you tomorrow."

CHAPTER 3

Elizabeth Goes Looking for Her Past

The very beginning was the place to start. Every story has a beginning and an end. Elizabeth had bypassed her beginning and had seemingly started her life in chapter 2. Now she realized she definitely needed to return to chapter 1 if she was going to discover how the story ended.

Elizabeth knew very little about her past. Her mother had been very reluctant to discuss it. Anytime the topic came up, it seemed to make her mother more than just a little uncomfortable, so Elizabeth long ago stopped asking. She did know a few things. She had been born in Kentucky. Her adoptive mother had told her that much. She knew she was born in a home for unwed mothers in Louisville, Kentucky. That was the extent of her knowledge about her past. That wasn't a lot to go on. Surely, such a home no longer existed. Those homes had gone out of service years ago, and whatever records they may have kept would have long since been destroyed; but that was the first chapter in her book and her first record of life. She had to start there somehow.

She thought she had been placed in foster care from that home and adopted when she was very young. Her adoptive parents had been wonderful. They had wanted children more than anything in the world and had finally managed to adopt two. They had loved her and devoted their lives to her and her adopted brother, Peter. Their home had been safe and happy. It had been filled with love and family of all sorts. She had never felt any desire to locate her biological past. She had parents, and she had a large extended family that she was very fond of. That had been enough for her until now.

She sat, drinking coffee at her kitchen table and watching the sun comes up. She had been unable to sleep. The whole scenario had played over and over in her mind all night. Now she sat there, sorting through everything she had learned thus far. There was this book she had written, some stranger who was actually a character in her book, and a place she had imagined that was real after all. It was a scenario that Elizabeth was having a hard time coping with. It would have sounded completely bizarre to anyone else, but oddly enough, it made sense to her. It was the "whys" and "hows" that were quite the mystery. The key to this whole thing had to be somewhere in her past. Some relative on her mother's or father's side had to be the Emily that Dan had known and loved and the one she was looking now for;

but which side? Both of her adoptive parents were gone now, so Elizabeth felt free to search for her past without feeling as though she was doing them an injustice.

The driving force behind this book had to have been someone from her biological family who, through some channel, was able to communicate without her realizing it was happening. She had never been aware of any contact, but that was the only explanation for much of what had happened. How else could she have described a meadow she had never seen or drawn a face she didn't know? Whoever the lady was in her past, surely she had met Dan in that meadow and had used Elizabeth and her meditation sessions to find him again. It was an interesting theory. The whole thing might have made another interesting book, but she wasn't interested in going down that road again. Writing one book was enough. Penning a second one wasn't anything Elizabeth was interested in doing. No, just searching the details would be engaging enough without having to put pen to paper to them. Besides, she wasn't sure she wanted the world to think she just might be crazy.

If anyone loved a good mystery better than she did, it was her daughter. It was early, but she picked up the phone anyway. Elizabeth smiled as she dialed the number. Rachel was going to love this one. "Hi, sweetie, did I wake you?"

"No, I always get up to watch the sun come up." The groggy answer on the other end of the line assured Elizabeth she had done exactly that.

"Awww, I'm sorry, Rachel. I have quite the story to tell you. I haven't slept all night, and I couldn't stand waiting any longer. Go back to sleep. How about I take you to lunch, or better yet breakfast, when you wake up?"

"Sure. Let me call you back when I come to."

"Okay. No hurry. I still have some more details to sort out before then anyway. Talk to you in a bit."

That was not like her to call anyone so early. She wasn't usually up that early herself. The trouble was, she was just busting to tell this whole thing to someone. She did have some thinking to do. She had been right, a lot of thinking to do, but she was feeling the need to talk this over with someone not involved in any way. She was interested to see what Rachel would think of all this, and she wanted someone to reassure her that she wasn't dreaming.

The meadow itself in her meditation must have been given to her without her knowing it. She had not dreamed up that lovely place as she had always thought. Someone had to have put a picture of the real meadow there in her mind. As uncomfortable as it made Elizabeth to believe that, it would explain the dress and hat. She had never put clothes on herself, but she had just appeared in that dress and always carried the hat. She had wondered about that hat, and why didn't she have shoes on? She had just assumed she didn't wear shoes because she had always loved to be barefoot. Now she was beginning to realize that what she had thought or envisioned about herself or the meadow really had nothing to do with her creation of this place. It would also explain why she never settled on the seashore. She had always loved the sound of the waves coming in and the gulls crying in the distance. Try as she might, she never managed to make the shore her peaceful place. Her mind had always come back to this meadow, so she just stayed there. The whole idea of transfer of thoughts would have frightened her if it had not been so intriguing. Even more intriguing was the idea that it wasn't just transfer of thought from person to person in a room but rather across a great span of time.

It gave her an uneasy feeling to think that her mind could be that open to ideas from anyone. Yet meditation was just the medium for such transfer. Hadn't she often tried to get into her daughter's mind years ago to be sure she was okay when she would be out late at night? Often she had felt successful, and when checking with her daughter, she had been right. She just never expected to be on the receiving end of thoughts from someone not even from her time. Now she was determined to find the one who could find her across time and get into her head.

Elizabeth was clueless as to where she should even start. She had read articles and seen shows where people had located their parents, but most of those had been done through the search program for adopted people, and her past dated beyond that data bank. It was a fairly new program that allowed children and parents to register if they wanted to find each other. She was sure her parents weren't looking for her so it wouldn't be so easy. Not all of the results were pleasant either. Some had not liked what they found. Some had been rejected or scorned. Some had found happiness. She was very apprehensive about what she would find. She wasn't really looking to gain a new family, only to find a past that seemed to be haunting her. She wasn't really concerned with being disappointed by what she found unless she couldn't find Emily, but the idea that she could open up old wounds that should have been left healed bothered her a bit. She had an adopted brother who had searched for and found his biological mother and, in the process, a whole new family. Once their adopted parents were no longer alive, he had immediately set out to find his roots. He had been quite satisfied with his decision, and his search had ended successfully and happily. Elizabeth was happy for him at the time, but she had no desire to follow in his footsteps.

Some people seemed to feel the need to connect to their past. Elizabeth had always lived for the day with no need to dwell on the past. Even though her father had once called her a dodo bird, she rarely spent much energy remembering or worrying about the past. The problem now seemed to be whether she was dwelling on the past or not; it seemed to be deeply involved with her present and her future. She had always lived each day and let tomorrow worry about itself, but now she suddenly realized that things were different, and she must face her past to find what or who the diving force was behind this mystery. The past seemed to be dictating her future, and if she was going to be the pilot, then she needed to know which direction she was supposed to be taking.

The oddest part of it all was having that seat next to Dan on the plane. No one in her past could have arranged that. Apparently he had been looking for her since the book came out with no success. Suddenly they are thrown together on an airplane bound for Charlotte. Not much could be any stranger than that. There just wasn't any explaining that one. At least she no longer believed he was pretending or making up some wild story to gain publicity from her book. She was convinced he was telling the truth and was honestly searching for answers to a very unusual mystery. Dan was looking for a lost love, but Elizabeth was searching for a ghost from her past that seemed to be haunting her. It was the only theory at this point that made any sense at all.

The next logical step seemed to be contacting her brother. They didn't talk often enough. He lived in another state, and they were both busy. An occasional phone call, an e-mail or two, and a few holiday gatherings were about all the contact they had managed to maintain in the last few years. She wondered now how they could have drifted so far apart. Maybe it was her move and the distance that separated them. Maybe it was her withdrawal from life after the death of her husband. Either way, it had happened, but he would know where to get started with the search and wouldn't even question why she was looking. This time she looked at the clock. It was eight o'clock now. He would have been awake for some time. Peter was always the early riser in the family. Once again, Elizabeth reached for the phone.

"Hey, Peter, how are you?"

"Great, sis, how are you? What is new with you? What are you doing up so early? Why are you calling me at eight o'clock in the morning? I thought you were the late sleeper. Say, I see that book of yours is doing nicely."

"My goodness, you ask so many questions in one breath." Elizabeth was amused. Her brother always had a lot to say in person, but on the phone he was usually brief and to the point. Maybe it was because she called so rarely, but more than likely it was that she never talked to him so early in the morning. "Okay, one question at a time. I'm fine, thank you. What's new with me is what prompted this call, and it is that book that is at the root of it all. I needed some information from you."

"I don't know how much information you will get this early in the morning but ask away. I'll try to be of some service."

"How did you find your birth mom? I would like to try and locate my relatives." Elizabeth didn't really want to do the usual chitchat today. She was in a hurry to get started on this search, so she was hoping he wouldn't ask too many questions. She didn't really have answers for any questions he might ask anyway.

"I wondered if you would ever do that. I figured you weren't going to make that journey. Some people never want to, and you have never seemed the least bit interest in looking."

"I never wanted to before, but something has come up; and I feel the need to find out whatever I can about my past and any of my relatives I can locate."

"What is going on?"

"It's something about the book I wrote and some of the details involved in it. I will have to explain the whole thing next time we get together, but for now I just need a start button from you, please."

"Sure, that's easy. The first step is to get a certified copy of your birth certificate. That will give you the name of your biological mom and dad. After that, it is a 'seek and ye shall find' operation. What does that have to do with the book anyway?" Now

Peter was involved. Maybe she should have never mentioned the book. It wasn't really a secret; she just didn't know yet exactly what to tell anyone.

"It's a long story. Apparently there is some connection between my past and the characters in that story I wrote. There is also some man here in Charlotte who may have had a relationship with someone in my family. That's what I am going to try and find out. Oddly enough, he showed up on the plane ride home in the seat next to me last week. The whole scenario is way too complicated to explain over the phone. We must get together soon."

"It sounds fascinating. I can hardly wait to hear the details. If you need me to help you search, let me know. I got pretty good at finding people when I did my own looking. If you need help in Kentucky, let me know. I got pretty friendly with all the folks in the records office in a lot of towns there."

"I don't think I am actually looking for my mother but rather some relative of hers. Before I can find relatives, I have to find her, so that is where I need to start. Once that is done, I may be calling on you to search the family tree. I am sure I am going to need help there."

"Keep me posted on the search. Love you, sis."

"I love you too, Peter. Thanks again for the information, and when I get a chance I will fill you in on all the other details. When are you coming down here for a visit?"

"I don't know, but it sounds like I should be making plans to do just that if it's the only way to hear this story. Good luck with the search."

She hung up the phone. That was short and sweet, just like she had wanted it. She knew she should call her brother more often, but time always seemed to slip away from her. She was glad he hadn't pushed for details. She wasn't sure she knew exactly how to explain them to him just now. She was still sorting through it all herself, and she found it to be pretty unbelievable so far. No need to make her brother think she had gone off the deep end just yet. Certainly, it wasn't anything she could explain.

Elizabeth thought about her past. She had been born during the war. A lot of soldiers had girlfriends, made love to them, then went away, and never came back. Locating a family of a dead father might not be easy. Her mind was going in high gear over all the questions she needed answers for. It wasn't going to be enough to just locate her parents. She was sure it wasn't her mother who met Dan in that meadow, so she had to somehow go back to grandparents or great grandparents or aunts or cousins. That was going to make the search even harder. She had seen shows on such searches that had taken years before completion.

Her phone was ringing. She came back to reality with a jerk. "Hi, Dan. No, you didn't wake me. I have been up all night; and, yes, dinner would be wonderful. I have some progress to report too."

"Don't tell me you already found your parents."

"No, nothing like that, but I do have some pointers on getting started. I will just wait and tell you over dinner. It's not so hot that it can't wait till then. I talked to Peter, and he has given me an opening assignment."

Dan's voice suddenly sounded deeply concerned. Elizabeth sounded determined but tired. "Are you sure you are going to be okay with this search? I have decided I can accept the dead end if any of this is going to hurt you. I always thought I would make any sacrifice to find out what happened to Emily or who she really was, but seeing you sitting there in the meadow made me feel it isn't really all that important. It was a long time ago, some twenty years now, and there really isn't any need to cause someone hurt by opening it up again."

Elizabeth was firm and confident. "No, I think I need answers even more than you do, Dan. I will be fine. I have no expectations about my past. I just want information, not love. I'm not looking for a family to replace the one I had. I'm looking for a relative that might be a key to all that has happened in the last few months. That will make the whole process easier. I had love from my parents and plenty of it, and I adored them in return. This is just a research project."

Dan thought he might work on the love angle himself, but he wasn't going to say that just now. He had just met Elizabeth, but understandably, he felt as though he had known her all his life. "How about eight o'clock then? I don't think I can finish up before then."

"Eight will be fine. I might even have more to report by then. Please do not worry about this. I knew when I wrote the book that there was something strange about it. I enjoyed writing it very much, but I never felt like it really came from me, only from my hand."

"Whatever happens with this search, Elizabeth, I want to continue seeing you if that is okay."

"Yes, that would be very nice. For now, I will just meet you for dinner, and then we will make further plans."

"See you at eight."

CHAPTER 4

Making Plans for the Research

Rachel hung up the phone. She looked at the clock by her bed. Seven o'clock in the morning? Her mother was never up that early. Something must really been bothering her. She would have never called her that early if everything was okay. She pulled the covers over her shoulder and turned over to finish her night's sleep. She lay there thinking about how strange it was for her mother to be okay but call that early. Now she was wide-awake. There was no way she could just roll over and go back to sleep. She climbed out of bed, brushed her teeth, and grabbed her first cup of coffee. With drink in hand, she reached for the phone and redialed her mother's number.

"Mom, are you sick?"

"Oh, darling, I am so sorry. I don't know what made me call you so early. I had been up so long that I didn't realize how early it still was."

"It's okay, I don't mind getting up early. I just got worried about you even being up that early. Are you okay?"

"Yes. I am fine. I have volumes to tell you though. My life has been shoved into high gear, and, of course, it is all your fault."

"What? What kind of high gear? What did I have to do with it? How could it possibly be my fault?"

Elizabeth was laughing by now. "I will make you a deal. You let me buy you that breakfast, and I will tell you the whole story. I am desperate for someone to listen to a good mystery that has become my reality."

"I think I am a good ear. Are you planning to write another book? I would be honored to listen to the plot."

"No, I have no interest in writing another book. You know that, but this story would definitely make a great book, and I need to see what you think of it."

"Sounds like a good deal to me. I'm dressing now. You want to pick me up?"

"Sure, I am on my way out the door. See you in just a minute."

Elizabeth picked up a notepad and a couple of pencils on the way out the door. She was hoping her daughter would have some ideas about this whole thing, and she was going to make some notes about what to do next. She chuckled to herself as she drove along. *Wait till I tell Rachel there really is a Dan Kerr, and like the book said, there really is a meadow. She is going to be more surprised than I was.*

Elizabeth had been shocked, to say the least, at the sight of her meadow, but somehow she had always suspected that something was very strange about the story she had written. With no desire to write a book or become an author, this story just felt like it flowed from her fingertips. Her daughter had once commented on how many writers thought for months about ideas for books. She was very surprised when her mother had just written this one out. Elizabeth had never really confided to her daughter about her sleepless nights and all the images of the story that just seemed to come to her out of nowhere. She always wondered that maybe there was more to the idea of writing that book than she was ready to admit. Now that her suspicions had been confirmed, it was up to her to find the truth, and she was ready to do just that.

Rachel climbed into the car asking questions before Elizabeth even had a chance to say good morning.

"I can accept that your life has been pushed into high gear. That is the price you have to pay for becoming a famous author, but please explain to me why it is my fault."

Elizabeth smiled to herself as her mind went over the blame game we all play. Rachel was still single with no children. She had never experienced the blame sharing that came with child bearing. As a mother, Elizabeth was very comfortable with everything that had gone wrong in her daughter's life being her fault. It was one of the roles of motherhood she accepted willingly. If her daughter's favorite shirt was missing, it had always been her fault. If she had missed getting an assignment in, it had definitely been Elizabeth's fault. If someone had not liked her or excluded her at school, it had somehow been her mom's fault too. She was sure if the country had gone to war, or the world had ended, that would have been her fault too. Now it was great fun to turn the tables on her unsuspecting daughter.

"Yes, it is your fault. You are the one who insisted that I get this book published. It wasn't enough that I just write the thing and have it printed up. Oh no, I had to go and get it published. You were just sure that was the thing to do. It was your persistence that got this book on the market; therefore, anything that happens as a result of that book is your fault."

By now, Elizabeth was enjoying the suspense. She made her daughter wait until they had gotten to the café and given their order before starting with her story. Then, over several cups of coffee and pancakes and eggs, she tried to explain in as much detail as she knew the story thus far.

It took Rachel more than just few minutes to absorb the whole idea. Elizabeth was right. She was very surprised by the whole thing. She was probably more surprised that her mother would climb in a car and ride off to parts unknown with some strange man without telling her than the idea of a ghost from the past dictating a book.

"I still can't believe you just went off with someone and never called me to let me know you were going or who you were with."

"Me either, Rachel, but for some very strange, unexplainable reason, I felt completely comfortable going with him wherever he took me."

"So there actually is a person named Dan Kerr?"

"Yes, and there truly is a meadow. It is even more beautiful and peaceful than I had envisioned it."

"This Dan person believes some relative of yours may have been Emily, and she may have put the story of your book in your mind?"

"I think that is just about it in a nutshell. Apparently I look like what he believes to be an older version of his Emily. What do you think? Please tell me I am not crazy."

Rachel was still putting all the pieces together. "Surprised" would not be the word. "Stunned" would be closer to what she was feeling. Her mom had always just been her mom—nothing more, nothing less. She had been there when Rachel fell and skinned her knee. She had been there when Rachel came home from school in the afternoons with projects due the next day. She had been there when she suffered her first heartbreak, and she had been there for every event in her life. She was just her mom.

Then suddenly, one day, her mom was not "just a mom anymore." She was an author and someone Rachel shared with the rest of the world; but more than that, she was now entangled in something that could only happen in the movies and never to Rachel's mom. She was having a hard time coming to grips with the whole concept, but she knew it definitely should be investigated. By the fourth cup of coffee, she had adjusted to the fact that there had to be something worth investigating in all of this. She didn't think that her mother had made all this up, and she believed that whoever Dan was, he had had an unusual experience. She disliked the feeling she had, like they were living in the twilight zone, but she did find the idea of solving this intriguing mystery. She was ready to go searching with her mother for the past that seemed to be dictating her life.

"Well, Mom, I feel sure you are not crazy; and I am certain you need to find your past, so let's get on with this search. I can hardly wait to find out what this is really all about. It looks to be a long search since more than just your parents are involved here. It will be harder to get a complete family tree. Are you scared?"

"No, not scared, but maybe "apprehensive" would be more proper term. I never was one to look back, not even to the past years of my life, let alone the past years of someone else's. I always felt as though looking forward was much more productive than looking backward, but now I don't feel as if I have a choice."

"Do you think it is your father's side or your mother's?"

"I know it could be either, but for some reason, I am leaning toward my mother's side. I don't know why I feel that way, but it's a pretty strong feeling. I am going to try to locate them both, but my money is on the maternal side."

"Okay, I guess you are right then."

"Finally, before I died my child said I was right. What am I right about?"

"It is my fault. I accept full responsibility." Rachel had gotten over the initial shock of the whole scenario and was now enjoying the mystery of it all. "So is there anything I can do to help in this search?"

"I was hoping that you would keep it on your mind, and if you come up with any ideas about how I could find these people, let me know. I have lots of help. Your uncle

Peter is in standby mode, and I know Dan is very anxious to be included in this search since it is his lost love we are looking for. I knew you would enjoy a good story, especially if it included an investigation. Your part really was to hear me out and respond in some sane way. I was beginning to think I might have lost my mind."

Rachel laughed at her mom. "You seem sound enough to me. It is one strange story; but I was there at the beginning of the book, remember, and I watched it develop, so I have to acknowledge that something real is going on here. What about Dan? What kind of person is he?"

"He is very nice. I thought first it was all just a publicity stunt. You know I have had several people who have pretended to be that character, but when I saw the meadow, I knew in my heart that it was something much more than that."

"How do you feel about him?"

"Interesting you should ask. I feel drawn to him for some strange reason. I feel like I have known him forever, and I guess I have known him a lot longer than I realized. I envy Emily and his love for her. Even as I was writing the book, I thought how wonderful it would be to find someone you love that much. I guess everyone who reads a love story has that feeling. I loved your father, but after the initial burst of love, we settled into what I like to call a comfortable relationship. Very few people actually experience what Dan and Emily did. I am hesitant to become involved with someone who is in love with a ghost, especially someone I already feel something for. I'm afraid by the time this is done, I will be very sorry to see him leave. Still, I certainly am willing to help him gain some closure in any way I can. At this point, it seems that his closure is my closure as well."

"Is there a reason you can't see him after you find this Emily?"

"No, but I think once he had found out who Emily was and what happened to her, his interest in me may fade. For now, I am just going to enjoy his company and try not to fall head over heels in love with him like some giddy teenager."

"Since you were right, and this is my fault, I can't possibly let you pay for breakfast."

Rachel picked up the bill, and they headed for the door. "Let me know how this goes. I expect a blow-by-blow account. Oh yes, and next time, please don't go riding off anywhere with a strange man without letting me know. You realize how risky that was I am sure."

"Yes, I know it was foolish. First, I was sure it was okay, then I was sure he was crazy, and then I knew it was okay. I feel quite safe and peaceful when I am with him."

"I have work all day, but I will be done by four this afternoon if you need me then. Just keep in touch from now on, please."

"I will, sweetie, and again, I am sorry for getting you up so early. It won't happen again. Thanks for breakfast and a willing ear. I was hoping that besides listening, you would have some ideas later when you had time to think it though."

"It was worth it to hear this story. I definitely need some time to digest all this. I have a few friends who might be able to help you with the search. Let me think about all this and get back to you."

"That would be great, but keep in mind that I would not like for anyone else to know about the reason for my search. I was sure that went without saying but just in case."

"No danger of that, Mom. I'd never reveal any of the details. I doubt anyone would take me seriously anyway. They would just think I was testing out a new book plot on them. When all this search is over, I expect you to put it all in your next book. Now you be careful. And call me later."

"I will. I promise updates for you daily from now on. Thank you for breakfast and have a great day. I am having dinner with Dan tonight, so I will check with you tomorrow; but don't hold your breath for that book."

Elizabeth left her daughter and drove slowly home, thinking through again all that had happened. She had been surprised when she decided to write a book. She had not been surprised when her daughter insisted she have it published. Her daughter had always been one of her strongest supporters, but Elizabeth was sure the little book would just sell a few copies to her friends and family and then be lost on the shelves. Quite the opposite had happened. It had magically materialized into a best seller and then was made for TV movie. She had been amazed when so many people had bought the book, but there was no description for what she felt now.

Dinner with Dan was in a quiet out-of-the-way spot. Elizabeth felt like a giddy teenager again. The two of them sat with their heads very close together still comparing notes on what really happened to Dan and what she had written about. Not all of the details were the same, but many were. She watched his face as he described his moments with Emily. He had such a frown and sincere look melded together. She wondered how she had ever thought he might have been seeking publicity. It was becoming more and more obvious he was a very private person.

"I hope you realize I have never told anyone before you about all this."

"No one would have taken you seriously anyway," Elizabeth answered, laughing more to herself at the idea of the whole thing than at Dan.

Now he was smiling as well, amused at the idea of trying to convince some of his friends or clients that he was involved in time travel. Telling someone about the whole thing would have been out of the question. "I don't think I really believed it myself fully until I read your book. I knew it was real when it happened, but once it was over, I began to think I must have dreamed the whole incident. The further in time I was from those meetings, the more I doubted myself. Still, I was never willing to sell off the meadow or change it in any way."

"That was a wonderful choice in my opinion. I was thrilled to see my meadow in all its glory. I was hoping you would take me back someday or at least give me the directions on how to get there and allow me to go back myself."

"I would do both. I will take you back any time you want to go, and I will allow you to go alone with directions. I know that it is a spot for you where being alone is a good thing. I can understand that. You can be rest assured that it will always be there in its original state. I did that for Emily all these years; now I will continue to do it for you as well as for Emily."

"Thank you, Dan. That is the nicest thing anyone could ever do for me."

The evening came to a close for the two of them. Elizabeth had never really gone to sleep the night before, and Dan had work the next day. Still they lingered. Each of them were hesitant to leave the other. Neither knew what the future held, and neither of them were willing to let the closeness of the moment die.

"I won't wake you in the morning, but please call me sometime during the day and let me know if you hear anything."

"You would be the first to hear, Dan. I will call even if I don't hear. Thank you for the wonderful evening. I haven't enjoyed myself so much in a very long time. I don't think I will know anything for a while yet. I am still trying to decide how to start."

"I know. I'm sorry. I think now that I have found a link to my experience in the meadow, I am just anxious to gain the closure I always thought was hopeless."

"We will find it, Dan. We will find it together. I am just afraid it is going to take a very long time. Parents might not be impossible to find, but people often spend years on a family tree. We will have to be patient and see it through no matter how long it takes."

Even as they reached Elizabeth's front door, Dan was slow to move. She finally dismissed him with a warm embrace and a kiss on the cheek. She forced herself to move away from him and go in the house. She closed the door and leaned against it. The urge to reopen it and rush outside into his arms was almost overwhelming. It was hard not to invite him in, but she was exhausted; and hopefully, there would be other nights. Even though she was tired beyond her limits, she had hated leaving Dan. Elizabeth didn't believe in love at first or second sight. She believed love was a passion that grew like a beautiful flower. First, it was planted, then watered, fertilized, and tended until it grew into a beautiful thing. This was different. She felt as though she had known Dan more than the short span of time since the plane ride. Surely with all the details of his love for Emily and hers for him, it made them more than casual acquaintances.

Dan drove home deep in thought. Elizabeth looked very much like Emily, but she was a special person all by herself. He didn't know how they had ended up together on that plane, but he was thankful every day since it had happened. Emily had gotten away from him. There was nothing he could have done about that. She lived and died in a different time and a different world from his, but this lady was in his day and his time; and if there was any way possible, he was not going to let her get away from him. He wasn't going to be pushy, he decided, just persistent. He would definitely call her tomorrow and the next day and the next.

CHAPTER 5

Following Leads

Elizabeth followed her brother's directions. She called the state capital and located the birth records department. It was just as simple as he had said it would be. All she had to do was send in a ten-dollar check, and they would send her a certified copy of her birth certificate. It seemed like such a natural thing to do, but it was very scary. She wrote out a short note merely describing what she wanted and what her name was. She wrote out the check for the ten dollars and put them together in the envelope. She dropped it in the mail that afternoon. Such a simple thing—to send for your birth certificate; but the minute Elizabeth dropped the envelope in the mailbox, she had misgivings about doing so.

She felt the need for some reassurance, so she called Dan.

"Well, I have taken the first step. The check is in the mail for the birth certificate. That was certainly easy enough to do, so why do I feel so doubtful about doing it?"

"Now you are making me feel guilty. Even easy things sometimes take a lot of courage."

"I'm afraid there is nothing left to do for a while but wait. It is done."

"Waiting isn't all bad. I have to be out of town for a couple of days, but I'll be back on Wednesday. I need to go back to my home office and make arrangements to be gone for a while. I want to stay in Charlotte so I will be available for you in case you need me. How about dinner at six o'clock on Wednesday? I should be back by then."

"That sounds great. I will look forward to it. Truthfully, I will be glad to have you around. Thanks for making such arrangements. I know that won't be easy for you. Have a safe trip."

Elizabeth tried to stay busy for the next few days. She poured herself into her artwork with a vitality she had not known in weeks. She finally finished all the barn pictures for her calendar. Now it was just a matter of selecting which ones would be included and which ones eliminated. She would take all the finished pictures to Rachel before going to the printers and let her select the ones she liked the best. Then she would get them off to the publishers, and that would be that. She was relieved to have that project finished before she got too involved in this new one.

It took the state only ten days to get the information out to Elizabeth, but it was the longest ten days she could remember in quite some time. She had a lot to do but found it very hard now to concentrate on anything except the hunt for her past. The one thing she did manage to do easily was getting better acquainted with Dan.

He had gone back to Detroit and made arrangements to be gone from that office and stay in the Charlotte office for the next few months. He said it was because he was hoping to be of some help in her search, but in truth, he was feeling some serious connections to Elizabeth. He was reluctant to leave her alone in Charlotte with this search in front of her. He was the cause of the whole thing, and if it didn't go well and she needed someone to be there for her at the end, then it was going to be him.

He was anxious to find out if Emily was in her past and, if so, then who she was and more about her. The striking similarities between Elizabeth and Emily made him even more determined to find out what had happened. He felt a driving need for closure. Before Elizabeth's book, it was a wish he had. Once he had found the book, it became a driving force in his life. Emily had just stopped coming to the meadow and had left him with nothing but a sad heart and a lot of unanswered questions. He was sure he would never understand how she appeared in the meadow, but he would like to know for sure why she stopped appearing.

Dan and Elizabeth had started their relationship with vigor. They had been meeting for dinner several nights a week and even an occasional movie or lunch. He was quiet, polite, and charming. How many nice things could you say about one person? Elizabeth found him to be all of them. No wonder Emily had been so taken with him. She was starting to feel very much attached to him herself. Elizabeth envied the deep love they had known. It must have been a very deep and wonderful love to have kept him from ever loving again. She worried that she was way too fond of a man in love with a ghost. He tried very hard not to push for answers or act overly apprehensive, but Elizabeth knew how she would feel if the shoe were on the other foot, and she found him utterly charming in his attentiveness.

Dan had made arrangements to stay in Charlotte for many reasons. He told Elizabeth that if he was to be of any help, he could stay. That of course was true. He told himself he wanted to be there the minute she found out anything about Emily. That of course was true as well. What he didn't put a voice to was the feeling he had for Elizabeth. She was fun to be with—kind, considerate; she was a lot like Emily yet very different. He found himself wanting to spend more and more time with her. He had known from the moment he saw Emily moving across the meadow that there was never going to be another woman for him, and yet here she was. Likewise, he knew the minute he saw Lizzie there on the plane, sleeping in the seat next to him, that this was the woman he was going to go any lengths to get to know and hope to keep.

He had a lot of work yet to do in Charlotte as well. He had stayed away much too long. Coming back there always made him think of Emily, and without her, it was always a slightly painful trip. He would often go to the meadow and sit for several hours at a time just watching the water and remembering. Consequently, he never got as much done there as he needed to. Now, if the phone would ever quit ringing long enough for him to get some work done, his stay would be worthwhile.

"WHAT?"

"Dan?" Her voice was a combination of question and hurt.

"Oh sorry, Lizzie. This phone has driven me crazy today."

Funny he would call her that. No one was allowed to call her that. The only person in her whole life that was allowed to call her that was her brother. As children, he had called her that to tease her and she hated it; but eventually, it was his term of endearment for her, and she enjoyed hearing him say it. That was the first time Dan had ever called her by that name. Still, it sounded so natural; and she didn't want to stop him from calling her Lizzie, so she said nothing about it.

"I didn't need to keep you long. Just called to say I got it!"

"I'm never too busy for you, Lizzie. You got what?"

"The certified copy of my birth certificate came in the mail today."

"Great. That was sure quick. I have time for lunch if you want to talk."

"Yes, I was surprised at how fast it got here too. I was hoping you would have some time for me. I'll meet you at Gabe's. That will be quicker for you. I'll order while I wait for you."

"Can we make it around one? I was going to try and catch one of the local builders on his lunch hour. I have been trying to connect with him for months."

"That will be fine. I'll meet you at Gabe's at one. Thanks."

Elizabeth stood alone in her kitchen and studied the single piece of paper in her hand. There in black and white was her past. It wasn't just her past; it was her biological roots. It gave her an eerie feeling holding that piece of paper in her hand. She read it over and over again. She read it silently; then she read it aloud.

Father's name...Robert Norman

Father's home address..Memphis, TN

Father's occupation ....Teacher

Mother's name...Evelyn Hickman

Mother's home address ....Mayfield, KY

Mother's occupation...Secretary

Baby's name ....Marcella Sue Norman

Funny how that felt, standing there, holding a paper that told her all that information. It didn't look like a lot on the piece of paper, but it spoke volumes. Suddenly she was someone other than herself. Here was a whole different person with a different mother and a different father. Until that very moment, she had never thought of her self as anyone but Elizabeth Scott. She had a family with aunts, uncles, and a host of other relatives. She had had a life and an identity. Now, she, with the arrival of this small innocent-looking piece of paper, was someone else. She had another mother, another father, and another whole set of relatives somewhere whom she didn't know;

and of course, they had no idea that she existed either. She had a different name as well—Marcella Sue. Funny how you can come into the world as Marcella and end up as Elizabeth. It gave her an odd sense of disconnection. Was she really Elizabeth? Or had she grown up as someone she didn't really know? Maybe all these feelings were exactly why she had never wanted to open up this door.

She had some reservations about delving into the past. Rejection was one possibility she faced. That would be okay. Surely her mother had given up her baby and moved on with her life. Whatever prompted her to take that action was history, and she would have made a new life and let the old one go. How would she feel if suddenly some sixty-two-year-old stranger approached her and announced, "Hi, I'm your daughter." Horrors of horrors! If her mother had wanted to find her, she would have done so long before now. Rejection, she decided, was not a problem. She expected that.

Somehow she felt very detached from this past of hers. It was much like researching facts for a book. That was what it felt like, not an emotional upheaval but a cool calculating research project. She found it interesting that she could feel that way. Suddenly as she continued to look at that small piece of paper, her life came back into focus, and she became Elizabeth Scott again. She was once more the person who was helping out a new friend. The fact remained, and that was exactly why she was researching her past. It was research for a book and a friend. It had to remain just that for her to be okay with the hunt.

Elizabeth arrived at Gabe's a few minutes before one and had lunch waiting when Dan got there.

"Now that is what I call service." He was even smiling as he pulled up a chair. He didn't do that often. Elizabeth was sure that he had high hopes of success with a birth certificate and the name of a mother and a father now.

"How does it feel, Lizzie? Are you okay with this so far?"

"Yes, interestingly enough, I feel very solid and secure about this. It was disconcerting when I first opened it, but now I am feeling totally okay with the whole plan."

"We could still call off this hunt if it is going to cause you any pain. You know I do not want anything like that. I have grown very fond of you in the past few weeks, and I would be devastated if I were the one to cause you any stress or heartache."

"No, Dan, it is fine, really. I felt a little strange when I first read my name as someone other than me. It was a very strange sensation to see another mother's and father's names in writing; but now I have adjusted, and I am just fine with it."

She showed him the piece of paper. "What do you think? We might be able to find the father, but finding a mother with only a maiden name to go on will be a little trickier. How do you find someone with only a maiden name to look for? Surely sometime in her lifetime she moved on, found a new love, and married."

"I am sure you are right. I never thought of this search as being so complicated. I foolishly thought you would just open up a magic book, I guess, and find your parents the next day."

"What do you think?" she asked. I don't know any other way to locate her without doing some legwork. I think to go to her hometown and start there would

41

be the easiest way. I am familiar with Mayfield, and it is a small-enough town to do legwork in."

"That sounds like a good idea to me, Lizzie. Would you like for me to come with you, or would you rather go alone? I could take a few days off and make the trip. I won't push, but I would love to come along."

"I think I need to do this alone, Dan, if you don't mind. If I come up short, I want time to feel sorry for myself and be disappointed without burdening you for a while."

"I understand, Lizzie, but if you need moral support, just let me know. I will be as close as your cell phone. Please remember you wouldn't be a burden. We are in this together."

"Thanks, I will be calling often, I am sure. I was hoping that you might do some legwork from here on locating my father while I am gone. You could do some of that from here, I think. At least you could get us started on his side, and if we need to do legwork there, we can do it when I get back from Mayfield."

"That's true. I will plug in your father's name tonight on the computer and do a search. You can take the mother. I will do the computer work on the easy one while you are gone. At least if he's married, his last name wouldn't change."

"That would save me some time. I never had been too good with computer searches anyway. If you have no luck at all, then once I return from Mayfield and rested a week or two, I will head to Memphis and see what I can uncover there."

Dan wasn't happy about letting her go on this venture by herself, but he understood why she felt it was the right way. He wanted to be there for her to share in her disappointments or her successes, but he didn't feel he could insist on going if she would be more comfortable without him. The truth was, he would miss her terribly while she was gone. He had become accustomed to her being around. He had not felt this way about anyone since Emily. He would never have believed he would feel this way again about anyone, especially someone he had known such a short time; but somehow, he felt he had known Elizabeth for a lifetime.

She had given him his own job in this project, so he would set about his task of locating Robert Norman and remain steadfast on the other end of his cell phone in case she would need him. She smiled at the seriousness in Dan's face. "Your job is like the princess in the tower. You can't come out of your room until this man is located."

"Oh, I won't; you can be sure of that."

Elizabeth left her brother's phone number with Dan in case he had trouble. "Peter has done this before. If you have any trouble, give him a call. He is like a bloodhound; once you put him on a trail, he just won't quit. His curiosity is aroused already, and he knows that I am looking, so you may have to give him a few more details than I did; and I'm sure he would be honored to help in the search. More to the point, he may be insulted if we do not include him."

"I will put in a call to him before I even start, Lizzie. He might come up with something I would miss."

They had one last cup of coffee and lingered as usual, not wanting to part. Finally, Elizabeth made the move. "I must get going, and you need to get back to work. I have to pack and get some rest. It is a long drive, and I need to prepare myself mentally for this one I think."

"I know. I am just having a hard time letting you go on this journey alone. I still feel as though I should be there with you."

"Honestly, Dan, it is going to be okay. I am not nervous or afraid of what I will find. It is simply a research project. I will stay in constant contact."

"All right, but if you change your mind, all you have to do is whistle."

They left the restaurant, and each headed to their own home deep in their own thoughts. Elizabeth was busy thinking through what she would need on the trip and what she would find. Dan was equally occupied worrying about what she would encounter.

Elizabeth packed up enough to be gone for a week. As an afterthought, she packed her camera. She was sure Kentucky would have some wonderful barns, and as long as she was there anyway, she might as well make the trip work for her. She was very apprehensive about this trip but very excited as well. She had high hopes of finding the answers to all of her questions as well as Dan's. If she hadn't found out anything by the end of the week, then she would come back home and regroup.

Driving was something she had always enjoyed doing. It seemed to give her time to clear her mind and let her think through whatever was bothering her. This trip would be no different. She definitely would have plenty to think over.

Rachel came by early the next morning before her mom left. She wanted to hear any updates her mom had found. "Sorry, Mom, I have been quite busy at work and haven't even checked in with you the last couple of days. How is it all going?"

"Now who is up early?" Elizabeth laughed at the sight of her daughter. She was still in her pajamas and no makeup. She knew Rachel must have just crawled out of bed and driven over. "How would you like a cup of coffee before I leave? I am glad to have you see me off."

Elizabeth showed Rachel the birth certificate, which identified her as another person. Her daughter studied the piece of paper a few minutes before saying anything. "Marcella? Are you okay with this?"

"Yes, sweetheart, I am fine. I think the search will be fun actually. I have a wonderful family and great memories. Nothing could ever change that. I am searching for information, nothing more. I will be fine."

"Would you like for me to come with you?"

"No, thank you, dear. Dan offered to do that as well, but I really think I need to go by myself. I won't be gone long, and I will call you every day and give you an update. I wanted to keep as low a profile as possible. The drive will give me thinking time."

"Yes, that is probably a good idea. No need to announce to the town what you are looking for."

"Not exactly, I am going to just pretend to be looking for friends of my mom. She was from there as well. That should make my cover easy."

"Well, if I can do anything from here, just let me know. I will be on standby as well. She looked over the barn pictures, made her selections, and offered to take them to the printers. At least, she said she could do that much. It would make her feel as though she was helping.

"Thank you, Rachel. I will keep in close touch and update you daily."

They had one last cup of coffee and a quick conversation. Elizabeth loaded her suitcase in the car and headed out. She spent the whole day on the road. The drive was long but uneventful, and it gave her hours of time to think. The book, the meadow, the mystery, her past, and Dan—they all ran together in a whirl. Her mind never had an idle moment the whole trip.

She arrived around suppertime, found a motel, checked in, and went to get herself a bite to eat. Mayfield was a typical small Kentucky town. She had been here often as a child. Her adoptive mother had also lived in Mayfield. Although her grandparents had died before Elizabeth was born, she had an aunt and uncle who had lived there while she was growing up. Elizabeth had stayed a few weeks every summer with them, so coming back now was almost like coming home. The town, of course, had grown since she had been there last. She didn't recognize much of anything, but she had expected that. It still seemed small enough to accomplish what she needed.

It was very strange that both mothers had originated in the same town. She wondered if they had even known each other and if there was some connection between them. They must have been at least close to the same age. That long ago, the town would have been small enough that it was very likely everyone in town knew everyone else. She finished supper and headed back to the motel. The drive had been long, and she had to make some phone calls before she went to bed.

"Hello, Dan. I made the trip just fine."

Dan was very relieved to hear her voice. He had worried all day about her driving that far alone and her emotional state as well. "Hi there, Lizzie, I am very glad to hear from you. It's a long trip alone. Do you have a plan yet?"

"I am staying in the Holiday Inn South in room 224. Well, actually, it occurred to me that someone from each high school class is responsible for keeping in touch with the alumni for class reunions. Surely there is someone here that does that. I am planning to go by the school tomorrow and see if anyone would know who that person might be for the class of 1921."

"Wow! I would never have thought of that."

"I have a few other ideas and options that might work as well. I will see how many of them I have to use to obtain our information."

"It sounds like you did some hard thinking on the road. I have to tell you something."

Elizabeth didn't know if she liked the sound of that or not. Dan was always serious, but he sounded really serious now. "Uh-oh, what is it?"

"I really miss you."

"Whew! I thought something really bad had happened. Funny you should say that because I really miss you too. By the time I was an hour out of town, I considered turning around and coming back to get you. I was sure you were busy working so I dismissed that thought and drove on."

"You knew I would have taken off work in a heartbeat and gone with you. I asked, but you didn't want me."

"That's not true. I did want you; it is just that I was afraid of what I would or wouldn't find. I wasn't sure I wanted to share defeat with you, and I didn't know if I could bear seeing you disappointed either."

"I thought we were in this together."

"You're right. We are. I will keep in touch. I'm going to get some rest now. Tomorrow is going to be a very long day. I am sure."

"Okay, Lizzie. I will be thinking about you. Call me please. Night, love."

Elizabeth called Rachel as well to report in and let her know she had arrived safely. She explained her plan and promised to report in as soon as she learned anything at all. Now with the entire duty of phone calling taken cared of, she was sure she wouldn't sleep a wink; but after the nine-hour drive, a long hot bath, and a cup of tea, she was fast asleep.

Chapter 6

Her Own Hometown

Elizabeth was up early the next morning. Sleep had not been easy all night, and she had awakened before light, unable to sleep again. She poured herself a cup of coffee and picked up an apple Danish before approaching the desk clerk at the counter.

"I was wondering if you could give me directions to the high school, please. I am trying to locate some old friends, and I am hoping to find the information I need there."

"Certainly I can. It isn't far from here. Of course, nothing in town is far." The clerk drew out a small diagram for Elizabeth, which included the courthouse and the local high school. "Good luck with your search. If I can be of further service, just let me know."

"Thank you, I will."

She arrived at the school just after eight. She had planned to arrive after the classes had started, and the halls would be empty. She went first to the library to see if they, by some chance, had old yearbooks. Her hunch was right. She found the one from 1921 and sat in a chair to look through it. She found Evelyn Hickman right away. She felt her mind reeling. She had never expected to find her so easily. Yet there she was, staring out at Elizabeth from the pages of that old book. She searched the face for any familiarity but found none. There were some similarities though. Her mother looked tall with long dark hair. She thought probably she had her mother's eyes as well. Beyond that, either she looked like her father or someone else besides her mother in the family. Dan had said she looked like Emily, whoever that could be. It definitely wasn't her mother. Funny, she had wondered if she would feel some kind of connection to this person who had given her life and then given her up; but no matter how hard she stared at the picture, she felt nothing. That was a good thing, she thought.

There was something more interesting than her biological mother in the picture that caught her eyes. There was another face in that graduating class that stood out in the crowd even more than Evelyn Hickman. It was a face that took her breath away and made her heart race. That could not be possible. That face could not have possibly been in that picture, but there it was—her mother, her adoptive mother. She had graduated top in her class, and the second highest classmate was none other than her biological mother. Elizabeth sat in the chair, staring at the picture and the information, unable to move or continue on for the moment. So they had definitely known each other. Now

46

the question remained: was it possible that her adoptive mother never really knew who her biological mother was? No, that would not be possible. Had they been friends?

It was all too coincidental. Now she was really feeling uneasy about opening up this can of worms. Elizabeth realized that Mayfield must have been a very small town, and certainly she had expected the two women had known each other; but being friends or being in the same school and class was something she had never considered. She was unsure as to how she was feeling now. She felt her face flush. Somehow she felt that she had discovered some deep secret that she shouldn't know and was afraid she might get caught. She was glad she didn't have anyone with her. It was hard enough for her to adjust alone to this latest bit of information. It would have been harder with a company. Before the day was over, she would adjust and accept this latest development as just another piece in the puzzle to be solved.

She finally regained her composure. She made photocopies of all the pictures in the yearbook that included both women and then headed for the office. At least this would make her job slightly easier. To ask questions about a class her mother was in would not seem nearly so strange, and to locate some of her friends would seem even less unusual. The woman who greeted her at the counter was young and friendly. She had a strong Kentucky accent and that wonderful helpful spirit that could still be found in small towns. Elizabeth explained to her that she was doing some family research and asked if she knew who would be the person in charge of locating alumni for the class of 1921.

"My mother was in that class, and I was trying to locate some of her friends and relatives here in Mayfield. I was hoping that there would have been someone in charge of notifying each class for their reunions. If there is, then they would have had addresses and phone numbers of the other members of the class."

"Oh, how nice; that sounds like a fun thing to do. I believe there are two people who take care of contacting that class—Madelaine Hines and Roberta Cullverson. Madelaine's daughter works here in the office. Let me get her for you."

The daughter, who came out from the back office, was just as helpful as the first young woman. She heard Elizabeth's story and was instantly ready to help. "My mother is at home this morning. If you have time and would like to stop by and see her, I will call now and tell her you are on the way."

"That would be so helpful if you would. I am only going to be here a few days, and the faster I can get on this, the better it will be. I am taking some time off work to do this, and I'm afraid I don't have as much time as I would like. Thank you so much."

That, of course, wasn't the whole truth; but Elizabeth didn't want to waste any time she didn't have to, and she did truly need to get back home and get busy on her work. What she didn't tell the woman was that she actually had two mothers in that same class. That would be a little difficult to explain but nowhere near as complicated as the true reason she was on this search.

Elizabeth called Dan on the way but got only an answering machine. She was disappointed, but she left a message for him to call her when he got time and then called Rachel. She just couldn't hold this news until evening. She had to tell someone.

"Mom! Did you find out anything?"

"I have uncovered at least one revelation. Are you sitting down?"

"Should I be?"

"Yes, I think so. In fact, even if you are sitting down, you better hold on to something. Both my mothers were in the same class here in high school."

"What?"

"Yes, you heard it right. My biological and adoptive mothers were both in the same class. In fact, they graduated first and second in their class."

"Wow!" There was a long moment of silence on the other end of the line.

"Is that all you can say?" Elizabeth laughed at her daughter's lack of words. She had felt the exact same way as she gazed on the picture that told a story yet to read. "I warned you that you should be sitting down."

"What more can I say? Are you doing all right?

"There was a moment there when I thought maybe I wasn't; but, yes, I am over the initial shock now, and I am fine."

"That is incredible. So have you found her yet?"

"No, I am on my way to talk to someone who might have information. It is one of the ladies who is in charge of notifying members of the class about alumni gatherings. If anyone knows where she is, this lady might. I am at her house now. I will call you later this evening."

"Okay, Mom, good luck there."

Elizabeth pulled up in front of a small white home in an older part of town. Her aunt had lived not more than three blocks from here. She must have known her as well as her mother.

"Mrs. Hines? My name is Elizabeth Scott. Your daughter called and told you I was on the way."

"Yes, please come in. I don't get many strangers for visitors these days. How can I help you?"

"Thank you. I won't take up much of your time, but I was looking for some information, and I was in hopes you might have that."

Elizabeth followed the older woman into her sitting room where she had laid out tea and cookies. "I don't have the chance to entertain much these days. I hope you have time for some refreshments. Now, how can I help you?"

Elizabeth explained to her who her aunt and mother were. Mrs. Hines had known them both well. "Your mother was quite the star of our graduating class, you know. She was the youngest and the smartest. Your aunt was quite a bit older. I didn't really know her well, but she lived not far from here."

"Thank you, but now I am looking for this woman." She had made a photocopy of the graduating class, and she pulled it from her purse and pointed to her biological mother. "I understand they were good friends, and I would like to ask her some questions. Do you know how to contact her?"

"That is Evelyn Hickman. I lost touch with her personally several years ago, but her sister lives not far from here. Let me give you her address and phone number. She will be able to put you in touch with Evelyn I am sure. Of course, she has gotten quite strange lately, so maybe I should give you Mary's address as well. There were three of them."

"Three of them?"

"Yes, your mother, Evelyn, and Mary. The three of them were always together, always competing, and always into something. I will give you Mary's address and phone number as well. She might be able to answer some of your questions about your mother as well if Evelyn can't. You will like Mary. She is quite the colorful character."

"Thank you, you have been most helpful. Mother passed away last year, but I had a desire to do some family research and find out more about her friends and family."

"Mary lives just a few blocks over from me, but you might try Evelyn's sister first."

"Thank you, I will check with them both."

Elizabeth took the paper with all the information from her and got back in her car. She sat there almost in a daze. It seemed all too easy. She had expected to search for years to find some trace of a family she had never known. Instead, she had found them in a few hours. She didn't know if the sister knew about her or not, but she doubted if her mom had ever told anyone. She drove to the address without calling ahead. She thought the element of surprise would work better in this case. She wondered what Mrs. Hines had meant about her aunt becoming strange lately.

It was an older home. The yard was full of plants and flowers. The porch had the usual old-fashioned swing, and there was a picket fence surrounding the whole scene. The grounds, while small, were in need of work. Elizabeth took a deep breath and walked up to the door.

The lady who answered was about the same size as Elizabeth with dark eyes and gray hair. Before she could say anything, the woman stepped out onto the porch and closed the door behind her. She was looking hard at Elizabeth. "Do I know you from somewhere?"

"No, I don't believe so. I am from Charlotte, North Carolina. I am here trying to locate some old friends of my mother. I understood that your sister and my mother were very good friends, and I was hoping to find her to ask her some things about my mother." Elizabeth was showing her the picture of the class, pointing to her adoptive mother and saying that she was looking for her friends.

The older woman was still studying Elizabeth with a piercing stare. "I must know you," she said. "You look so familiar. We had some relatives years ago in North Carolina."

Suddenly, Elizabeth saw a change of expression in her eyes. It was that look that told her the woman had connected with whoever it was she thought she knew. "Goodness," she said, "you look very much like a distant relative of mine. Who did you say you were?"

Elizabeth explained several more times to the woman about her mission, but somehow she wasn't getting anywhere. She only became more agitated and more suspicious. "I don't think I should tell you where my sister is without asking her first. If you will give me your phone number, I will give it to her; and she can call you if she decides to."

Elizabeth had the strong desire to just come right out and tell this woman who she was and what she wanted, but the poor woman was already obviously unset and nervous. There was definitely enough family resemblance that this woman was suspicious of Elizabeth's motives. That supported her theory that Emily must have come from her mother's side of the family.

There was nothing left to do but just leave her card with her aunt and move on. To tell her the truth would serve no useful purpose. The next stop would be the other friend, Mary. Hopefully she would be more informative. She suddenly realized it was past lunch, and she had not eaten yet. She made a detour for the main street and went some place to get food. Fast food had never been her favorite, but it would do for now. She was anxious to fill her stomach and get back to work.

While she was eating, she called the woman named Mary to see if she would be at home later and be available. Luck was with Elizabeth. When she gave a quick summary of what she was looking for, Mary was quite excited to see her old friend's daughter and invited her to come whenever she was ready.

Mary was a short, little plump lady with a quick smile and bright blue eyes. She was waiting for Elizabeth with a cup of warm tea and cookies. It was her second tea and cookie snack today. She was beginning to feel like Santa on Christmas eve.

"How wonderful," she said with a cheerful face. "I never expected to get to meet you. I lost contact with your mother, and I have often wondered how she was doing."

"Mother died a year ago, and I just wanted to gather some other information on her and her friends. Maybe even some experiences she might have had in school."

"I am sorry to hear that. You know she was my best friend in high school."

"Yes, I got that information from the school. The woman who is in charge of the alumni meetings said my mother's best friends were you and another lady named Evelyn. I went by her sister's house to see if I could locate her, but her sister wouldn't give me any information."

"I am not surprised. Did she look at you strangely?"

"Interesting you should ask that. She thought I was some lost relative looking for something she didn't want to reveal. I didn't really understand, but they told me at the school that she might be a little strange."

"I am not surprised that she would react that way to you."

Elizabeth had the distinct feeling that this woman knew more than she was telling. She wasn't sure if she should confide in her what little she already knew or just stay with the original plan and act ignorant of any connection. She decided that since the door was already open, she was going to just walk through and let whatever happens happen.

"Did you know my mother and Evelyn very well?"

"Yes, child. I stayed in touch with both of them for many years after graduation. The three of us were like the three musketeers. We went everywhere together. We had no secrets from each other."

There it was. The door was now wide open. There was nothing left to do but walk thorough. "Did you know that I was adopted?"

"Yes, and I believe you have an adopted brother as well."

"Yes, I do. Then did you know that my real mother was Evelyn?"

There was a moment of silence. Mary took a slow sip from her tea and looked as though she had traveled many years away in her mind. Elizabeth was wondering if she had misunderstood her meaning when she said, "We had no secrets."

"Yes," the answer came slowly and thoughtfully. "I knew. I was the only other person who did know. Evelyn never told anyone in her family. She was afraid of disgrace, but there is quite the family resemblance showing in your face, your build, and your coloring. I am sure her sister spotted that right away."

Elizabeth smiled, remembering the suspicious looks she had gotten at the sister's house. "Yes, she even said I looked like some of her relatives."

Elizabeth and Mary sat over their tea and cookies until almost suppertime. Mary told her the whole story of her conception, her birth, and her adoption. It was wonderful to find out all those details from someone not really involved in her life. She explained how she was the one who had been instrumental in connecting the other two when the situation arose and how it had worked out so well for all concerned. It was a time in history when a single, unmarried woman didn't fare so well in a small community with a child. The three of them had put their heads together and made a vow of silence.

Elizabeth shared with Mary the whole detailed story of why she had even started this search. She told of the man who was the main character in her book and the chance meeting on the plane. She even confessed her feeling for Dan to Mary. It felt good to be able to talk to someone else about this whole story besides her daughter and Dan. Mary was so easy to talk to and even more easy to listen to. She understood why her mother had considered Mary her best friend. Elizabeth felt as though she was talking once again to her own mother. She had forgotten how much she missed her and the hours they had spent discussing everything.

Elizabeth loved hearing stories about both of her mothers, and Mary had many of them. Their mishaps and successes during high school and growing up were of great interest to her. She suddenly realized how late it had gotten. "I am very sorry to have taken up your whole afternoon, but I have certainly enjoyed our conversation. I must say I appreciate your honesty and your valuable information."

Mary gave her the address and phone number of a nursing home. "I am afraid your mother has had a pretty serious stroke. She will not understand who you are or what you are looking for, I'm afraid. I can't help you with past relatives because your mother moved here from Charlotte when she was a little girl. Back then, families didn't do a lot of visiting back and forth. Whatever family she had there, I never met. She did talk about an Aunt Emily though. She encouraged her to pursue her art. You know your mother was a very good artist, and she always felt she owed it to her aunt Emily. I think she died young."

"Thank you very much. You have been so very helpful. I will go by this place tomorrow and see her at least. Not all of my questions have been answered, but you have certainly covered a multitude of them."

"I was glad to do it and even happier to have the opportunity to meet you."

"My heartfelt thanks for arranging all this and keeping their secret all these years. Not many people could have held their silence. Not many people are as good a friend as you have always been."

"Knowing they were both happy made it easier; besides, your mothers were just as good friends to me. It was an equal trade off. We loved each other and took pride in our honor and secrets."

"Just in case you have wondered all these years if you did the right thing, you did. I had a wonderful mother and an even better life. It was the best decision the three of you could have ever made."

"Thank you for that. I always worried about how it would work out, but it certainly seemed the right thing to do at the time."

Elizabeth drove away reluctantly. She had enjoyed the wonderful woman and could have sat talking to her for a much longer time. What a special friend she had been to both of them. It was amazing she could have kept such a secret in a small town all these years.

She dialed Dan's number again, and this time she reached him.

"Hi, Lizzie, how is it going?"

"'Interesting' would be the operative word, I believe."

"Really? Are you getting the answers you had hoped for?"

"I don't really know what I had hoped for, but I have found out a lot of information. I will just tell it to you when I see you. Let's just say it has been eye-opening. Meanwhile, my mother is here in town in a nursing home, and I am going to try to see her tomorrow. She has had a serious stroke. I am not looking forward to that visit. For that one, I could certainly use some support."

"I hate to say I told you so, but I tried to come along."

"I know. It is okay. I will get through it. I don't know that she can be of any help at all. The word is that she won't really be able to communicate well with me, but I will go out there and try to talk to her. Right now, I am going to get a bite of supper, then take a long soak, and go to bed early. It has been a really long day."

"Thanks for touching base with me, Lizzie. I have barely been able to work all day for worrying about how you were doing and feeling guilty for letting you go off alone. Call me when you finish at the nursing home, please. I will, at least, give you some words of encouragement from here."

She said good-bye to Dan, called Rachel, reported in to her some of what happened, and promised to give her all the details when she got home. She was tired and didn't feel like explaining to either of them all the long details she had discovered. The final step was still awaiting her, and she wasn't looking forward to that one. She had never liked nursing homes. She didn't like to see the elderly in such a pitiful plight for it made her think of what was ahead for her. She detested the smell of nursing homes and the absolute hopelessness of the residents within. Tomorrow was definitely going to be a test of her emotional stability. She had a quiet dinner alone in the dinning room of the hotel and headed upstairs for a chance to put all the pieces together in her mind.

CHAPTER 7

Father Located

Dan turned on his computer as soon as he got home. He was tired, and he had an early morning appointment, but sleep was not going to come just now. He was even more anxious than Elizabeth to locate her past relatives. He knew he wanted to find out who Emily really was and how this whole chain of events had happened; but the truth was, after just a few short weeks, he was deeply in love with Elizabeth. At first, he had thought maybe he only felt that way because she looked so very much like Emily, but now he was sure her looks had nothing to do with it. She did resemble Emily in looks and nature. They were both positive, happy people with a kind and gentle spirit about them, but Elizabeth was different in many ways from Emily.

He had been deeply in love with Emily some twenty years ago, and he never forgot how that felt. When that relationship ended so abruptly, he was sure he would never love that way again, and he had been right. Until Lizzie came along, no one had ever been able to take Emily's place in his heart; but now, for the second time in his life, he had that same wonderful feeling he had experienced in the meadow. Since the day he had seen her on the plane, he knew she was going to be important in his life, and he didn't want to let her get away. Now he was desperate to hold on to her. He had kept most of his feelings to himself. To profess his love to her now would only convince her he was still in love with a ghost. She would be sure he was simply substituting her for Emily. No, he had to find a way to convince her that Emily had nothing to do with his love for her.

For now, the only thing he could do was to help her in this search, and then when it ended, he hoped she would believe him when he told her the truth. Closure for them both would be a good thing. Hopefully, after that, they would be able to face the world together from that day forward. He was sure they would be permanently stuck in the past if they were unable to locate her parents and Emily, so his part in this now was of utmost importance.

He picked up the phone and made a call.

"Hello, Peter?" It was the call to Lizzie's brother that she had asked him to make. He was hesitant to call some stranger with personal business, but he did not want to offend either Lizzie or her brother.

"Yes, who is this?" The voice on the other end of the phone assured Dan that Peter had been asleep. He had been so zealous about his part in the search that he had forgotten that Peter was one to retire early. Lizzie had told him about her brother's sleeping habits, but in his haste to get this project started, that information just wasn't important.

"I'm sorry, did I wake you?" Dan looked at the clock. It was nine o'clock. He was such a night owl that it was hard to imagine anyone would be in bed this early.

"No, I have developed a cold, but I do usually go to bed quite early. I am an 'early to bed early to rise' person. Who is this anyway? Did you tell me that already?"

"This is a friend of your sister, Lizzie. I am involved in a sort of research project with her, and I was instructed to enlist your help."

"Lizzie? Wow! You must be a very good friend. No one but me has ever been allowed to call her that and get by with it. She was never much for nicknames. What did you say your name was?"

"Dan, Dan Kerr. I didn't know that. She never mentioned it. I didn't mean to offend her."

"Nah, she would have told you if it wasn't okay I'm sure. Say, isn't that the name of the character in her book? Did you make up that name?

"Yes, that's me; and, no, I didn't make it up. I believe I am the cause of all this research."

"So what did you need from me?" Peter was still trying to wake up and figure out who this stranger was and why he would be calling so late at night.

"You know that we are searching for her biological relatives in hopes that somewhere in her family there is someone I once knew."

"No, I haven't gotten all the details, but I knew she was looking for her biological parents."

"She got her certified copy of her birth certificate yesterday in the mail, and she has gone to Mayfield to search for her mother. She felt as though she would have more success by going directly to the town. She left me with the name and hometown of her biological father, and I promised I would do a search on the computer for him while she went looking for her mother. She said you were a bloodhound on these things, and that I should give you a call for help so I thought two heads would be better than one."

By now Peter was fully awake and understanding that this man was somehow connected with his sister's new desire to locate her past. His curiosity was definitely peaked. "Oh well, okay then, give me the information; and I will see what I can do from here, and then I will get back to you as soon as I find anything. I'm going to have to come there for a visit, I guess. I definitely want to hear the story behind all this. My interest is going to get the best of me. I can't seem to squeeze enough of the details about what is going on there from either of you to make sense from it all."

"Lizzie left early this morning. She was planning to be gone no more than a week. She thought if it took more time than that, she might reconsider her actions. Maybe sometime next week you could come down. I am anxious to meet you too. I have heard a lot about you, and I'm sure Lizzie will have even more to tell you by then."

"I'll check the calendar and see. That sounds like a great idea. I haven't been to Charlotte in a while. Where did you meet Lizzie?"

"Accidentally, I ran into her on a plane. It is such a long and complicated story that it almost requires a face-to-face to tell it all. This story is so far out that I think you have to see the person telling the story to actually believe they are telling you the truth. Lizzie said I might have to give you more details, but I'll just invite you down, and we will have an information party when you get here."

"That sounds like an offer I won't refuse."

Dan gave Peter the information he had and his phone numbers as well as his e-mail address. He sounded as nice as Elizabeth. He was sure he would like him and was even more anxious to meet him in person. By the time he got off the phone, he was very encouraged. Maybe Lizzie did like him too more than he knew. After all, didn't she let him use her nickname that no one was allowed to use but her brother? He started the coffee going. It was going to be a long evening. He was a little startled to find himself smiling.

He sat down with his coffee and started his appointed task. He found the network search for individuals and typed in Robert Norman. The computer offered up a multitude of Normans. Dan started down the list, reading each one. There were several pages of them. They were scattered through every state in the union. What if he was listed in the book by initials or a middle name? That would really complicate things. This was going to be a long night. Dan never realized how many people could have the same name. There were 1,678 people in the United States named Robert Norman. He read through the first few pages, then took a sip of coffee, and let out a loud frustrated sigh. Suddenly he had an idea. He picked up the phone and dialed zero.

"Could you give me the area code for Memphis, Tennessee, please?"

Then he dialed the Memphis area code and the information number. Elizabeth had been a war baby. There were two very possible scenarios. Her father could have been killed in the war and that was why she had been put up for adoption. If that were the case, he would not be listed among the living. The other option was her father never knew about her but did come home. Many years ago, people were not generally as mobile as they were now, nor did they seem to have the urge to move about the country. There was a good chance that if he made it through the war, he simply would come back to his own hometown, settle down, and would still be there. Dan got the Memphis information operator.

"Could I have a number for a Robert Norman please?"

"I don't have a Robert Norman listed in Memphis, but there is one in Bartlett."

"Where is that?"

"It is a small town close to Memphis. It is still in the Memphis area code. Would you like that number?"

"Yes, please, that would be great, thank you."

Dan took the number. He couldn't believe how easy that had been. He glanced at the clock. It was almost nine thirty at night. It was probably too late to call anyone now, but he didn't feel like he could wait till morning. He was shaking as he dialed the number. Could this possibly be her father? Would it be possible for him to be found so easily?

There was an answer on the other end, "Hello."

"Mr. Robert Norman?"

"Yes, this is he. Who is this?"

The voice sounded very strong and healthy. If this were Elizabeth's father, he would be almost eighty-five by now. Surely this couldn't be him. Dan's excitement over his great success was slipping in to disappointment.

"I am sorry. I think I have the wrong Robert Norman. The man I am looking for would be in his eighties. I'm afraid you sound much younger than that."

"I will be eighty-five in December, but thank you for the compliment. Who is this?"

"My name is Dan Kerr. I am looking for a Robert Norman who was a teacher in Memphis before the war. He and my father were in the service together."

Dan didn't know what to tell him. He had not expected to actually reach Elizabeth's father in such a short time, and he had not formulated a cover story for his call. It was a bit unusual to be calling someone late in the evening to tell them they had a daughter they didn't know about. Besides, that wasn't Dan's place to do. His job was simply to locate the father, nothing more. It was the best cover story he could think of on the spur of the moment.

"I was a teacher in Memphis before the war. I only got to teach a year before I joined up; but when my tour of duty ended, I came back and took up the banner again. This time I chose to live and teach in a smaller town close to Memphis. After the war, I didn't like crowds much. I taught until they made me retire, but I don't remember any soldier buddy named Kerr. That doesn't mean anything though. There are a lot of places, people, and things I don't remember these days. How is your father?"

Dan's own father had never been in the war and had died some years back after a long illness. It was a good cover story though, and now he had no choice but to play it to its finish.

"He is doing very well, thank you. He has good days and bad. I wanted to locate some of his buddies from the war for him. I thought it might give him a boost to have the chance to hash over old times. Your name was on his list."

"Yes, sometimes that is a good thing; even though they weren't all good times, it does help us to talk to each other about them. Just have him call me anytime. I am around here most of the time now that I am retired. It would be nice to hear from some of the old gang."

"Thank you, sir. I will tell Dad that I reached you, pass on your phone number, and let him get back to you. I was just doing some legwork for him, looking up a group of his old buddies. Have a nice evening, and thank you for the information. Sorry to have disturbed you so late."

Dan put the phone back in its cradle and sat there stunned. He couldn't even believe that had just happened. Nothing could be that easy, yet there on the scratch pad beside his computer was the phone number of a man who, sixty-three years ago, had fathered a child, with or without knowing it; and Dan just happened to be in love with that child.

It was very late now for Peter to be up, but Dan called him back anyway. This was too good to keep till morning.

"Hi, Peter, it's Dan. Wake up. You aren't going to believe what just happened."

Peter just happened to still be awake. He too had been reading through the Robert Normans. He laughed at the idea that he might not believe something. With all the strange calls and information he had been getting from that end, he wasn't going to be surprised by anything now. "Go ahead. Just try me."

"I just talked to Lizzie's father."

"Okay. You are right. I can't believe it. How did you do that?"

Dan explained to him what happened. Peter was more than just a little surprised. "What is that old saying about the apple falling from the tree? I guess Lizzie's father just fell by the tree."

"Sure looks that way. I will call her and give her the news. Then, it will be her choice to call or not to call. At least that part of the search is over. Thanks for being willing to help, and I hope to meet you sometime in the near future."

"You bet. You know, they always talk like it is impossible to find parents, but it didn't really take me much longer to find mine. I will get hold of Lizzie myself and see what her schedule is like as well. Then I will make plans to get down there. Have a great night and thanks for including me in this business, whatever it really is." Peter laughed and hung up. He was definitely going to Charlotte.

Dan had done his work there. Now his thoughts turned to Lizzie in a strange town all alone looking for her past and dreading what she might find. He was missing her and wishing he had not let her go alone on this mission. He was afraid it was too late now to call her. What if she was exhausted and had gone to bed. He would not want to awaken her. Before he could dial the number, his phone rang.

"Lizzie, hi, how was your day?" Dan was very relieved to hear her voice on the other end of the line.

She had called to report in what she had found that day. She sounded lonely and tired. More than that, she sounded scared and unsure as to whether she wanted to continue this search.

"I guess I am okay. This has gone quicker than I expected, but certainly there have been some unexpected turn of events. Tonight I am tired and not sure I should have opened this can of worms."

"I was afraid that might happen. You have my permission to abort the mission and just come home. I no longer feel like it is necessary, and I definitely don't like hearing you sound this way."

"I have gone too far now to abort. After a good night's sleep, I will be fine. I have just never liked nursing homes, and I dread going there. Besides, I'm afraid it will be a fruitless venture. From all I can gather, my mother is going to be no help at all."

"You need to do whatever you feel is best for you. Just please call me when you leave the nursing home and let me know you are okay."

She had been so preoccupied with the challenge of facing her real mother in a nursing home that she had forgotten to ask about his progress in his search for her father; and Dan, hearing the hesitancy and dread in her voice, forgot to tell her too. He was feeling very guilty for letting her go off alone. After all, it was his fault she was even involved in doing this.

Dan logged in back and checked some flights for the next day. If he left very early in the morning, he could be in Mayfield by midafternoon or at least in time for supper. If he flew up there, he could ride back with Lizzie. He could get in there by three that afternoon if he left out early. At least, if she was completely overwhelmed, he would be there for her when she got back to the hotel. He made the reservation and packed a suitcase. He couldn't get there in time to go to the nursing home with her, but he just wasn't going to let her come back to an empty hotel room alone after such an emotional afternoon. He knew in his heart that wasn't the only reason. He was missing Elizabeth terribly. He didn't want to be in Charlotte another minute with her somewhere else. Besides, he told himself that he should tell her the news about locating her father in person rather than over the phone. He set his alarm and went to bed. The next day would be a wonderful surprise for Lizzie but a long day for him.

CHAPTER 8

Mother Located

The mother she was searching for was finally found. The information her mother's friend had given her was correct. The River's End Retirement and Nursing Home was the last stop on a long search. Elizabeth pulled into the front parking lot and got out of the car. She looked around. The facility was a very pleasant-looking place. It appeared to be fairly new, she thought, and quite large for such a small town. She swallowed hard, opened the door, and entered the home. The lady at the front desk was pleasant looking and greeted Elizabeth with a warm smile.

"Hello, I am Mrs. Bennet. Are you needing information on our facility today or just visiting someone?"

"I am looking for a woman named Evelyn Hickman, please. Could you direct me to her room?"

"I have not seen you in here before to visit her." The lady eyed her with a great deal of suspicion.

Elizabeth was sure she was not going to give her the room number, so she thought it best to reveal the story behind her search. She didn't enjoy feeling like a spy or a criminal because she was looking for a mother she had lost, but she could understand how unusual that must seem for some stranger to suddenly show up wanting to visit.

"One of her good friends sent me here. Her name is Mary McCord. Apparently she and Mrs. McCord and my mother were very good friends. I am sure this must seem very odd, but I was adopted when I was a child, and I have reason to believe that Evelyn is my biological mother. Her age, her birthday, and all the other information points to her. A close friend of hers from her hometown gave me this address and said I could find her here." Elizabeth produced the original birth certificate she had been carrying in her purse.

"I have had something interesting come up in my life, and I was hoping she could shed some light on some of my relatives. I had not wanted to infringe on her life, only enough to look into my past relatives."

"Oh my, how interesting. Yes, I know Mary. Who was your adoptive mother? I am sure I knew her as well."

Elizabeth gave her the details in a nutshell of her life and updated her on her mother. Of course, she had known her, and she was sorry to hear that she had passed on.

"I doubt that anyone knew about you. There is no mention in her papers of another daughter."

"Another daughter?" No one had mentioned to Elizabeth that she had a sister. Not even Mary had told her that in the whole afternoon they had spent together. Of course, she had given Elizabeth only the information about her past, not her mother's. She was right to not mention a sister. That was for Elizabeth to find out for herself and not for Mary to tell.

"Yes, Mrs. Stamps has a delightful daughter who faithfully comes here every Saturday afternoon promptly at one to visit her mother and tend to her needs. She has not missed a Saturday in the last two years."

"Could I visit my mother?"

"Certainly, you may. She has had several strokes, and there are only a few moments when she seems quite lucid; but most of the time, she doesn't appear to know anyone or be aware of what is going on."

"Thank you, I do not think it would be necessary to tell her who I am. I only hope to get some background information from her. I will try not to tire or excite her. I had thought to only ask her questions in the context of searching my own mother's past, but now I realize that would expose my identity. I will do what I can to keep it light."

"She is in room 215, down the hall and to your right. I am sure you will do fine. Please let me know if you need anything further."

"Thank you, I will. Please, I am sure this goes without saying, but I would prefer you not reveal to anyone what we have discussed here this afternoon. I think that information would serve no useful purpose as public knowledge."

"No need to worry. I would never say anything. I hope you can find what you are looking for."

Elizabeth walked slowly down the hall toward room 215. The facility was like many others she had been in. This one was clean, neat, and pleasant looking. The walls were decorated with bulletins about upcoming events, paintings and drawings done by the occupants, and pictures of the residents all in assorted arrangements. She had never seen that done before, and it gave the place a special personal touch. Even the smells were not the unpleasant ones Elizabeth usually associated with nursing homes.

There it was! Room 215. Her final stop. Elizabeth felt some serious apprehension. She stood outside the door and took a few deep breaths. This was her final test. Unsure of what she would find, she peered slowly around the door. The woman she saw looked smaller than she had expected. She was propped up in bed surrounded by several pillows and was talking to herself. Elizabeth tapped lightly on the door, but getting no response from the occupant, she pushed open the door and entered. As she walked slowly into the room, the woman seemed unaware that she was there but continued to mumble to herself.

She pulled a chair up close to the bed so she could study the older woman more closely. She had snow-white hair and dark brown eyes. She had expected the old woman to look like her, somehow, or at least closely resemble her, but she didn't see many similarities. Maybe that would have been hard for Elizabeth to see, or maybe her mother just looked so different sick and in bed. Her left side was immobile, paralyzed. Elizabeth assumed the stroke had caused all her problems. One side of her face sagged, but her gaze was direct. As their eyes locked, it went through her mind that here was a woman who carried a child for nine months and then gave it away and never looked back. She looked like a normal little old lady. Somehow Elizabeth expected her to look hardened and hateful. She leaned forward and softly spoke to the older woman. "Hello, Mrs. Hickman? My name is Elizabeth."

"Aunt Emily," the old woman replied. Her face brightened, and she almost had a smile. "It has been so long; how wonderful of you to come and visit me. I have been drawing pictures for you. Would you like to see them?"

The woman's voice was strong and clear, but Elizabeth was sure the old woman did not know what she was talking about. Maybe she resembled some relative of hers. After all, this was her mother lying here, and it would not be unusual for her to look like part of the family; but her mother did not know that. Suddenly it dawned on Elizabeth what she had just missed. Emily—wasn't that the name Dan was seeking? This could definitely be the connection they had been searching for. Dan had said she looked strikingly like Emily.

Elizabeth was firm but gentle. "No, my name is Elizabeth, Elizabeth Scott. I am visiting here from Charlotte. My mother was a friend of yours, I believe."

"Why did you come to visit me? I have not seen you since I was a child. You never came to visit us before." The old woman was sitting up straight in bed now and was looking straight into Elizabeth's eyes with a stare that seemed to go to her very heart. The smile turned to a frown, and the look in her eyes became one of mounting fear, but Elizabeth did not know why. She had said nothing more to the woman.

She chose not to respond to the last statement but continued once again, "I am Elizabeth Scott, and I am looking for some of my family members. I was hoping that you might have known them."

By now, it was obvious that she was becoming extremely agitated. "Liar!" the old woman screamed. "You are dead. You came for me, didn't you? I can't go yet, Aunt Emily. My daughter is coming back to see me." The older woman's eyes had taken on a wide stare, and she was now screaming as loudly as she could and starting to shake uncontrollably.

Elizabeth didn't know who or what Emily was, and she was sure this conversation was about to end in disaster. She quickly left the room and crossed to the nurse's station. "I am afraid I have upset her terribly, but I don't know how it happened. I am powerless to make it better. I said nothing. She seemed to think I was someone she once knew. I was hoping she would know some of my family, but I don't seem to be able to communicate with her."

"It's okay, dear. She often gets excited. She will be fine; don't you worry. I will go right in and settle her down. Perhaps it would be best if you didn't try to talk to her again until another day."

"I was told she has a daughter who comes every Saturday afternoon to visit her. Do you know her name?"

"Paula Sue Stamps is her name. She is a dear soul who is very kind and tender with her mother. She usually arrives promptly at one o'clock and leaves sometime after four. Perhaps she could help you find whatever information it is you are looking for."

"Thank you. Yes, I am hoping that is the case. I will come back on Saturday."

Elizabeth left the nursing home quite shaken and headed back to her hotel. It had been an emotionally exhausting afternoon, and she felt the need to just get away from the search. A quiet corner somewhere and a cup of coffee was what she needed now. She flipped open her cell phone and dialed Dan's number. It was midafternoon and catching him this time of day might not be easy.

He answered on the first ring. "Hey, Lizzie, how are you doing so far?"

Elizabeth was so glad to hear his voice. She didn't realize how much she would miss him, and she didn't know she would have wanted him with her on this search as much as she did. "Hi, Dan, I think it is going well. I just had a dreadfully frightening experience here at the nursing home. I don't think I was ready for that one. I have some updates for you, but I sure wish you were here. I'm headed back to the hotel to have some coffee and think through all this. It would taste so much better with company."

"I would have been with you, but you asked to go alone, you know."

"I know. I had no idea how this would play out. I thought it was something I needed to do alone. Now I think it was something I should have involved you in."

"That's okay, Lizzie. I'll get the details from you after you have had your rest and coffee. Just call me back whenever you are ready to talk. I'll be waiting. You know I miss you more than I thought I would."

"I miss you too. I'll be home as soon as possible. I am pulling into the hotel parking lot now. I will call you back in about an hour."

"Okay. Talk to you then."

Elizabeth parked the car on the side and went in the front door. The restaurant looked pretty much deserted, which was exactly what she was hoping for. She found a back booth and ordered a cup of coffee. She gazed thoughtfully out the window and lost herself in the events of the past few days. She had gotten the information about her mother and located her much easier than she ever imagined, but now she still had a few last hurdles to cross. Should she go back to the nursing home and try again with her mother or just wait and tell some stranger that her mother had given birth to a child before her and had given it away? It didn't look as though she was going to get far with her mother in her present state, so unfortunately if she was ever going to finish this search it was going to have to end with her sister.

"Excuse me, is this seat taken?"

The voice brought her back to reality. Her heart leaped. That voice. "Dan! What are you doing here? I just talked to you, and you didn't mention a thing about being here." She had clamored out of the booth and was hugging him as though she wasn't ever going to let go. She didn't want to ever let go, and he was hugging her back with the same feeling. Somewhere in the embrace, Elizabeth felt tears gushing down her face. Where did they come from? She didn't realize how badly she had needed to cry.

"Hey, has it been that awful? I never meant to put you through anything this bad." Dan was starting to feel dreadful. He was responsible for this entire outburst, and he wasn't sure what she had discovered that caused it. He was at a loss to know what to say; but he did know how to hold her, so he just held her and held her. Eventually he released her, and they sat down to exchange information.

"No, really it hasn't been that bad. I don't know where that all came from. Just tension, I guess, from the whole search."

"I am so sorry, Lizzie. I should have never asked you to do this. It was totally selfish on my part, and now I have caused you great pain. I never meant to do that. I definitely should never have agreed for you to come here alone."

"I needed to do this, Dan. Honestly, it has not been terribly painful. Let's have coffee, and I'll fill you in on all the details."

They sat over coffee for quite some time while Elizabeth told Dan all the details of her search and her encounter with her mother. "There is definitely someone named Emily in my mother's family, and she must have been her aunt because she called me Aunt Emily."

"If she was my Emily, then I can understand why she called you that. You bear a striking resemblance to her."

"Would it be possible for you to stay till Saturday and go with me to meet my sister? I know that's a lot to ask, but I don't know if I can face her alone. I think I might need someone to be with me."

"You bet. I made arrangements to be gone from the office as long as I needed to. The work will still be there when I get home. I wouldn't miss this for the world. I got you into this, and the least I can do is stand by you through it."

"Well, we have all day tomorrow to wait. Maybe we could take some back roads, and I could take some barn pictures while we are here. I have seen some really great ones, but I didn't take the time to stop."

"We can do whatever you would like. Your wish is my command."

"Then let's go up to the room and rest. I would like a shower and some dinner."

Elizabeth insisted Dan to stay in her room with her. She had two double beds, and she saw no need for him to take a separate room. Besides she was anxious for the company. He had no argument with that request. The closer to Elizabeth he could be, the better he liked it these days. The evening went by quickly. A quiet dinner and a walk around the area gave them plenty of time to exchange details of their searches.

She was glad to hear that Dan had located her father so easily, but she was sure that the answers they were looking for were right here in Mayfield. She didn't know that she wanted to contact the lost father.

"Do you think there is any need to contact him? There could be an Emily in his family as well."

"Let's see how this one turns out first; then you can decide."

"I am almost positive this is where the answers are. I really don't believe he is going to be the key." She was going to let that one slide for now and just concentrate on the events here in Mayfield. Nothing else mattered right now.

What did matter was locked in Evelyn Hickman's mind, and Elizabeth would like to unlock that information for Dan. She wasn't sure her sister would know what she needed either, but now she was the only chance they had. The test ahead would come in convincing her sister that she was her sister and getting that information from her. That would take some charm and skill.

For now, she was going to relax and just enjoy having the day and Dan. The barns she

found in Kentucky were mostly gray or black barns. A lot of them were tobacco barns,

and many of them were in poor repair. Those were the ones Elizabeth saw as barns with

a lot of great deal of character. Those were the ones she loved the most. They found barn

after barn. Elizabeth had never taken so many pictures in one afternoon. The countryside was peaceful, and they seemed so far away from everything that was going on. The afternoon simply flew by. Elizabeth couldn't remember when she had been so relaxed and enjoyed anyone as much as she did with Dan. One more quiet dinner was just what she needed to calm her troubled soul. She didn't realize how lonesome she had been lately. She had not minded living alone at all. It seemed to suit her until Dan came along. Now she was beginning to wish he would stay forever. She knew how much she would miss him when he got what information he needed and was gone. He had said he was going to stay around after it was all over. Now she was hoping with all her heart that he meant it.

CHAPTER 9

Elizabeth Meets Her Sister

On Saturday afternoon, Elizabeth and Dan arrived early at the nursing home. They wanted to catch Paula Sue before she went in to visit her mother. They found the same friendly receptionist awaiting them.

"Hello," she smiled, "I have brought a friend who has been helping me with my search, and we are hoping to talk to Paula Sue. We won't bother her mother for fear of upsetting her."

"Oh, dear, she is fine. She does often take notions like that, but suit yourself. I have serious doubts that she would ever be able to help you, but you are welcome to visit her again. If not, there is a quiet lounge just down the hall. You can wait there and have some coffee while you wait. Her daughter should be here soon. She is usually very prompt.

"Thank you, would you tell her that we are waiting in the lounge and would like to speak to her before she goes into visiting her mother, but please do not tell her I am her sister. She has no idea, and I would like to tell her myself. It is going to come as quite the surprise, no matter who tells her."

"I would never dream of that. I will send her back there as soon as she arrives. Good luck with it all and your search. I hope Paula Sue can provide the information you are seeking." She went back to her office to continue her work. From where she sat, she had full vision of the lobby and the front hall. Elizabeth was sure she made a great watchdog.

Dan and Elizabeth sat almost speechless in the lounge, side by side on the sofa. The anticipation of what would follow made for little conversation. They were each lost in their own feelings, but finally Elizabeth realized she had been so deep in thought she didn't know when Dan had reached out and taken her hand. He was holding it tightly and seemed to be equally lost in his own thoughts. The warmth of his hand made her feel safe and comfortable. No matter what happened, she was very glad to have him there now. Why had she not wanted him to come when he was so much comfort to her?

She broke the silence. "Thank you, Dan, for coming here with me. I don't know what made me think I would want to do this alone. This last meeting would have been the worst."

"Probably the same thing that let me wave good-bye to you as you left alone. I wasn't thinking either. I guess my fear of interfering with your desires kept me from insisting on coming, but when I heard the despair in your voice on the phone, I knew that no matter what I had agreed to, I had to come."

"I'm afraid I have gotten very comfortable having you around. I am not sure now if I want to find this Emily person. I don't like the idea of losing you."

"You have no worries there, Lizzie. Whatever happens in this search, I have no plans to leave you. I feel the same, so you aren't going to get rid of me that easily."

Promptly at one o'clock, a dark-headed woman walked in. Elizabeth recognized the dark eyes and hair that was her own, but her facial features were Paula's mothers. There were a few similarities, enough she believed, that you could tell they were related but maybe not as sisters. She felt a surge of adrenalin rush and hoped she could remain calm and friendly through what was to come. She could feel her face flushing and her heart beating faster.

Mrs. Bennet leaned out the office door and greeted her. "Hello, Paula Sue. There is a couple in the lounge who would like to speak to you before you visit your mother. They wanted to ask you a few questions about some friends or relatives of your mother's."

The woman smiled a "thank-you" smile at her and turned toward the lounge to meet Dan and Elizabeth. She was closer now, and there were definite similarities between her and her mother. She was taller by possibly and inch or so than Elizabeth with a medium build. Well dressed with that schoolteacher appearance, she approached them with a pleasant-but-questioning look on her face.

"Yes, can I help you?" She didn't recognize either of these two people and had no idea what they could want with her, but she was friendly and courteous.

Elizabeth stood. "Hello, Paula Sue, please would you sit with us just for a moment? My name is Elizabeth Scott, and this is a friend of mine, Dan Kerr. We are from Charlotte, North Carolina, and are here in search of some answers from the past. We are hoping you will have some of the answers we are searching for."

"I don't know how I could possibly help you. I know no one from Charlotte, but I would be glad to try. How do you think I could be of any help?"

Elizabeth spent a few minutes explaining that she had recently become an author and what had prompted her to write the book. Then Dan took the conversation from there to explain how he had actually experienced what Elizabeth had written, and now they were both looking for answers together. "We have told no one else about all this since it is really such an unbelievable account."

"That is an amazing story," Paula said when they had finished. "I read that book and loved it. Are you going to write more? I still don't see how I can help you?" She found it flattering that such a famous author knew her name and was seeking information from her, but she was wondering to herself why they had confided such a story to her, a complete stranger.

Now came the tricky part. There just wasn't any way to tell someone that you were their sister. How unbelievable would that be for Paula to even entertain the thought that her mother could have given birth to another baby besides herself and then have given it away? She had lived almost sixty years as an only child with a doting and loving mother. Elizabeth started slowly. She explained how she had gone on a search into her background on request of Dan. "That search has led up here to this nursing home and your mother, Paula."

The look now on her face was one of doubt and suspect. "What could my mother possibly have to do with your search?" Paula was looking interested in their search but still totally unaware of what was coming next. She was making no connection that would explain their interest in her mother or herself.

"The simple truth is I don't know any way to say this other than just a simple statement. Your mother gave birth to a baby out of wedlock three years before she gave birth to you. She put that child up for adoption. There were only two people in this town who ever knew the truth. They were Mary McCord and my adoptive mother. You see, Paula, your mother is my mother too."

Paula had been semiattentive until now. Suddenly she was looking directly at her, but Elizabeth wasn't sure she wasn't just looking through her. She was ashen white and completely silent. Dan was poised to catch her if she fainted. He too realized what a shock that had to be as well. There was a long silence. Dan and Elizabeth remained silent, giving Paula time for what she had just heard to soak in. Slowly the color came back in her face, and she spoke.

"Why are you doing this? I have nothing you could possible want, and we don't have much money." The look on her face told Elizabeth that she didn't believe what she had just heard and was preparing for a fight.

"Please hear me out, Paula. I was a war baby. I don't know how it happened, but I do understand not wanting to rear an illegitimate child in the '40s, especially in a small town. Interestingly enough, she somehow managed to place me with an old classmate of hers. Mary McCord was, I believe, instrumental in making that happen. I'm still not sure how she managed to do that, but I am sure that she did. I have acquired a certified copy of my birth certificate on which the names of my biological mother and father appeared. There is no disputing the facts. I was born in a home for unwed mothers in Louisville. Once the baby was born and arrangements were made, I am guessing that your mother came home, back to Mayfield, and went on with her life as though nothing had happened."

Paula appeared to have recovered from the initial shock but was still poised for battle. As shocked as she may have been, she did not make any attempt to leave them. "What have you come here expecting to gain from my mother? She is barely aware of her own surroundings. I can't believe she could be of any help to you or any kind of mother to you now."

Elizabeth was calm and reassuring. "I have come expecting nothing. I am not looking for love from a mother or a family I lost or hoping for some great family reunions. I had a wonderful family, and I always would be grateful to my biological mother for giving me up for adoption. She did what she felt would be the best for herself and for me, and she was right. I had a wonderful life with two loving parents. I am simply looking for someone who I am sure was in my past, whose existence could explain what has happened in Dan's past and my writing of the book.

Paula was becoming calmer, but it was obvious she still had reservations about both Dan and Elizabeth. "Who exactly are you looking for?"

Dan was the first to respond. "Do you know if there was anyone named Emily in your past?"

Elizabeth joined in with an explanation and an apology. "I went in to see your mother on Thursday. I did not want to confront her about my adoption, but I did want to see her for myself. My adoptive mother and your mother graduated from high school in the same class. I had thought to ask her about some people in the class as a cover story. However, she thought I was her aunt Emily. Apparently she is dead, and your mother thought I was her and had come to take her home. I am sorry to say she got quite upset. I had no idea that would happen."

Paula thought for a minute and said, "My mother did have an Aunt Emily who died as a young adult from some type of congenital heart defect. In fact, I believe they lived in Charlotte, but I am not sure. I think that is where my grandmother moved from. That is all I know about her. I do have a trunk in my attic that belonged to her. There are some pictures of her in it, and the more I look at you, the more I realize you do bear a striking resemblance to those pictures. Perhaps what you say is true."

"Is there any way you would be willing to give the trunk to us or at least let us look through Emily's belongings?"

Paula paused for a moment. "I am sure what you are telling me is right, but still I don't know if I should give you the trunk."

Dan and Elizabeth looked at each other. They were both thinking the same thought. At last, their search had yielded success. Elizabeth pulled her birth certificate from her purse. She handed it to Paula. "Apparently it happened during the war, and your mother never told anyone, not even her own sister. I went to your aunt's house trying to locate your mother, but I never told her anything about this. I didn't come in search of a mother, Paula; I had one of those whom I loved very much. The truth is, Dan and the strange feelings I had when writing the book were the actual cause of this search. We came in search of some answers to some strange occurrences. We would appreciate any help you would give us. We aren't looking to make trouble or cause any grief, only to give some closure to our own lives."

Paula looked at the piece of paper for a long time. Elizabeth wondered how much adjustment it would take for her if someone had walked up and said, "Hi, I'm your sister." She thought Paula was doing remarkably well. She was very grateful that the woman was still sitting there talking to them. She truly had expected her to become angry and walk away from them.

"The trunk was in my mother's attic when I cleaned out her house. I don't know how or when she came in possession of it. I wasn't sure what to do with it, so I simply moved it to my attic when mother came here. I have never really gone through it. Let me think about all this. It is a lot to understand and deal with in one sitting. Do you have a phone where I can reach you?"

"Yes, I am staying at the Holiday Inn South, and I will also give you my cell phone number. I am only going to be here until tomorrow. I have been gone long enough, and I need to get back home and to work. If you decide later to let me have the trunk and its contents, I will be glad to pay shipping for it."

"Let me think on this overnight, and I will call you in the morning."

"I will look forward to hear from you. Thank you for hearing us out. It was nice to meet you. It isn't every day you get to find such a nice person who just happens to be your sister."

Paula turned and headed down the hall. She was late for her visit with her mother, and she needed to get away from Dan and Elizabeth and think about everything they had told her. She had some serious thinking to do and a lot to come to grips with. She entered her mother's room, crossed to her bedside, and stood there for a very long time just looking at her. How could she have carried a baby and then gave it to her best friend and never inquired about that child again? How could she have kept such a deep secret for all these years? Paula would have some adjusting to do.

It had been a long emotional afternoon. A quiet dinner in the hotel dinning room was what they both wanted. It gave them a chance to review what they had discovered and recover from the adventure. The meal started with simple chitchat. Neither of them was ready to think that their search could have come to a defeated end. Dan was the first to break the silence.

"Your sister seems to be a very nice person."

"She did handle that whole scene very well, I thought. I don't know if I would have been that calm and collected under the same circumstances. That is a lot to accept. The very idea that your mother would have had another baby before you and have given it away cannot be easy to believe. It is always easy to understand giving a baby up for adoption. That seems like such a good thing to do when the situation deems it necessary, but when it is your own mother doing the giving, then the whole picture changes."

"You know I never went down the hall and looked to see what your mother looked like."

"She looks like an older woman who has had a stroke, but Paula looks like a younger version of her. I didn't see much resemblance between me and her. Did you think I looked like Paula?"

Dan had to stop for a minute and think about that one. "No, now that you ask, I didn't see any facial similarities; but you definitely have her eyes and hair. Even her build, Lizzie, I believe you two were built the same."

"Do you think she will give us the trunk?"

"I think it is going to take her some time to adjust to the whole idea, and then I do believe she will let you have it. I don't really see any reason not to. The great aunt was not anyone she ever knew or had any attachment to. I can't see her refusing after she has had time to recover."

"I hope you are right. We have gone this far and managed to locate two parents in what I would consider record time. It would be a great disappointment if we were unable to obtain the trunk now. At least we think our search is over. There is no need to look into the other side of my family until we see what's inside that trunk. If I truly look like her then it is the right Emily. If not, then we will just have to resume the search after we see the trunk."

They went over and over the speed and accuracy of their search; then after one more cup of coffee, they headed for their room and a good night's sleep. The drive would be long, and they were both emotionally exhausted.

The last thing Elizabeth said before dropping off to sleep was, "Thank you once again, Dan, for being here beside me. I don't know if I could have done it without you."

"It was my place to be, and I wouldn't be anywhere else." She remembered hearing him say that and nothing more.

Chapter 10

A Sister's Gift

Elizabeth saw no reason to stay in town any longer. She had been there almost a week. She had talked to everyone she felt would have any information at all and everyone she could share her story with. It was over. She may not have accomplished what she came for, but there was nothing more she could do here. Now, it was time to resume her life in Charlotte. She had hoped that her sister would send the trunk with her, but that was Paula's choice, and Elizabeth would certainly respect that. She could also understand. Paula would want to, at the very least, inspect the contents of the trunk before giving it to someone else.

She and Dan had a leisurely breakfast at the hotel. She looked at him across the table from her. His frown didn't seem so deep, and he seemed to have a more peaceful look. They seemed to be so far away from the world of reality they both knew. It was peaceful here, and even though they had not been completely successful, they had at least found an Emily in her family.

"Are you going to be okay if we never see what's inside that trunk, or was all this for naught?"

"It will be okay, Lizzie. I have the most important part of the whole search sitting across this table from me. There would be nothing in that trunk that could be more important than that."

Elizabeth smiled at him. She felt the exact same way, but she wasn't sure just yet if she wanted to express complete surrender of her soul. "It sounds beautiful when you say that, Dan. I feel the same way. This search has been a wonderful research project, but my loved ones are you and my family at home in Charlotte. I am ready to go home and be with them."

They finished breakfast and went to their room to pack for home.

"Before we leave town, I would like to drive by my aunt's old house. I haven't had time to do that yet, and I had such good times there. It would be fun to see if it is still there and if it still looks like I remember it. The whole town is so very different that I'm not sure I can find it. The desk clerk will give us directions. They have been doing a good job of that. Do you have time for me to do that?"

"Sure, we have all the time you want to take. We aren't on any schedule, and it doesn't really matter what time of night we get home. We can go wherever you feel you need to go."

"I would like to drive by Mary's house and thank her once again for all her help. Without her, I would never had found my mother. It will only take a few minutes, and we can do them both on the way out of town."

"That's fine. I will call the office and check in. I need to let them know that I will be back on the job on Monday. Then I will be ready to go."

She could hear just a tinge of disappointment in Dan's voice. She felt it herself, but what more could she do? Perhaps Paula would change her mind later and let them know what was in the trunk. They loaded the car in silence and went in to check out.

Elizabeth asked for the directions to her aunt's and to Mary's again. The clerk wrote them out carefully on a note card for her. "I hope your stay has been satisfactory, and you have found what you needed to find. Oh, by the way, someone stopped in this morning and left this for you." The desk clerk handed Elizabeth a small envelope. The front was simply written Elizabeth Scott.

Inside the envelope was a note from her sister. Elizabeth's hopes soared. Maybe this was the answer she and Dan had been waiting for. Maybe the trunk would be theirs, and all the answers they had hoped to find would be within that box.

Dear Elizabeth,

I have considered your request. I do not think it is an unreasonable one to make. Under the circumstances, I feel that the trunk should be turned over to you. However, I would like to investigate the contents of the trunk myself before handing it over to you. I feel sure there will be nothing in the trunk that I would want to keep; but if I remove anything from it, I will give you a full description of what I have taken. I hope you will understand that.

Please realize that I am not trying to avoid all of this. It is going to take me some time to come to grips with all that you have told me. This has been one of the hardest things in my life that I have ever faced. Surely you can understand how I must feel.

I will ship the trunk on to you in a week or so. Please do not consider paying the shipping cost. That is my gift to you along with the trunk. I hope that someday we can have a long conversation and get to know each other better. I believe I would like that.

Your sister,
Paula Sue

There it was! The success of the whole trip was there on a small note card. She handed it to Dan without a word and waited for him to read it. Now that they had achieved their goal, neither of them felt fully satisfied. This whole adventure had started as a search for some lost relatives and someone lost to Dan years ago. Somewhere along the way, they had fallen deeply in love with each other. Now the search didn't matter at all. They had already found what they were looking for in the middle of the search. They finished loading the car and drove to the address for her aunt.

The little white house was still there. It looked exactly as Elizabeth had remembered it, only smaller. Of course, she had been smaller herself at the time. The little house with its picket fence and side garage seemed to remain untouched by time. Elizabeth was transported back to another time when she was a young girl, and life was simple. It was a time when she spent several weeks in the summer sitting by her aunt's side sewing and drawing. Those days seemed to be a lifetime ago.

"Would you like to ask the people living there if you could see the house inside?" Dan's voice cut through the memories of the past and brought her back to the present.

"No, I don't think that is necessary. I just wanted to drive by and see the place I spent so many happy summers. Going inside now would not be the same. I remember it being much larger and grander, but then, I was much smaller in those days."

"Then is it on to Mary McCords?"

"Yes, one last stop, and then I will be done. It was strange to see a woman who is, by blood, your half sister and have no feelings, one way or the other, for her. It was encouraging for me that she is such a nice person. If I have chosen a sister, it might have been her."

"It was kind of her to be willing to send you the trunk."

"Yes, it was very nice. Of course, she never really wanted the trunk. She didn't even know who Emily was, but it is hard to destroy or dispose of distant family possessions. This whole scene must really be hard for her to accept."

"I am sure it must be. She looked even more shocked when you announced that you were her sister than you looked when you realized you were sitting in your meadow. I tried to put myself in her shoes and imagine how it would feel to hear my mother had done that, and I had a sister out there all these years I didn't know. There just wasn't anyway I could envision such a thing."

Elizabeth smiled, remembering how amazing it had felt to look around her and slowly realize she had arrived in the most peaceful spot of her life, and it wasn't lost after all. "I think she might have been a more shocked. At least I knew the meadow in my mind all along. I knew what it looked like; I just didn't know it was real. She never saw this coming at all."

"That's a good point."

"It took a lot of courage for her to drive over here and leave that note. Just writing it and signing it 'Your sister' took a lot of nerve. I thought that was a nice touch. At least it means she is open to further dialog with me at sometime later."

"Do you want to have a relationship with her?"

"I don't know. I suspect not really as a sister, but I certainly wouldn't mind being her friend. She hasn't had much time to adjust, and yet she seemed to be taking it in stride. She doesn't really realize how much that trunk will mean to us, but she knows it is important, and she is willing to part with it."

"I wonder if she will remove anything from it before she sends it."

"Somehow I don't believe so. Now that she knows there are family secrets, there should be no reason to remove anything. I doubt there would be anything to remove anyway."

Dan's voice had an anxious edge to it. "How long do you think it will take to get to Charlotte?"

Now Elizabeth was amused. "You asked me that already. Are you getting a little anxious? I think not much more than a week. I think she will get it down now and go right through it; then send it on."

They stopped in front of Mary's home. "Come in with me. There is someone I want you to meet."

Elizabeth introduced Dan to Mary and explained that he was the character in his book who started all this. Mary smiled an understanding smile and offered them a cup of tea.

"Thank you very much, but we can't stay long. We wanted to stop, update you of what had happened, and say thank you once again for all your help. This would never have been possible if not for you. There was one small catch though. You never mentioned that I had a sister."

"I am not one to gossip or give unnecessary information. I was sure you would discover that for yourself."

"You were right. I certainly did. She is very nice. You have been a true and faithful friend to both my mothers all these years. You are a rare and precious gift that is not often found in today's world."

Elizabeth gave her a quick rundown on what and how she had gone to the nursing home and seen her mother. She told her of the encounter with her sister and the discovery of the existence of the trunk. She left Mary a copy of her book and promised to call her and keep in touch. They embraced like long-lost friends, and she and Dan got on the road headed for Charlotte.

Elizabeth called Rachel, gave her a quick update, and explained that they were on their way home. "We can have breakfast tomorrow morning when you get up, and I will try to give you every single detail I may have missed these last few days." Once that call had been made, she was ready to just settle in, relax, and let Dan do the driving.

"I am glad to be going home," Elizabeth finally said. "I am delighted this is over. When it started, I never thought it would be this emotional. Remember, it was just going to be a research project. Who would have known it would turn out to have such an interesting twist. Hopefully now I can concentrate on getting the calendar from the publisher and finishing up any last book tours. I am ready to be finished with those and stay home for a while. My artwork has been waiting for me, and now I have a whole new set of barns to give life on a canvass. I'm sure you are behind in your work as well."

Dan was glad too. Many times in the last few weeks as he had watched and listened to Lizzie, he had wished this had never started. Why he had been so insistent in opening up old wounds, he didn't know. It had been pure selfishness on his part and a flagrant lack of concern for Lizzie. He often wondered why an amazing relationship with her just wasn't enough for him. After all, he had the best of both worlds. He had Emily back and another wonderful woman rolled into one. For the first time in twenty years, he was interested in a woman. Why did he need to dredge up all of her past and his?

It was too late for wondering now. He had started the ball rolling, and it had come to rest here. Now it was almost over. The only thing left was to wait for the trunk and investigate the contents therein.

The trip home was peaceful and mostly quiet with both of them lost in thoughts all their own. Dan explained over lunch about his search for Elizabeth's father. In all the excitement of finding her mother, he had forgotten to give her the details of what made him think to call the operator.

"It was interesting how easy they both were to find. I would have never dreamed that we could have just located them both in a matter of days. You hear of those years and years of search that some people do."

"I would never have thought so either, but I am glad that was the case. I don't know if I could have stood all those years and years of search."

"Well, it is done now. I don't know if I should thank you or not for pushing me into doing this. I was able to see for myself my biological mother before she died; and I have found a sister I never knew I had, so it hasn't done any harm, I don't suppose."

"I certainly hope not. I don't want that on my conscience all my life."

"No worries. All is well. Now the only thing left to do is to wait for Emily's trunk and see what treasures might be inside it. I hope there is something for you, Dan. That would definitely make the whole venture worthwhile."

"I wonder how long it will be before she ships it."

"I am guessing not long. You will be the first to know when it arrives. If I forgot, I want to say thank you for coming to my rescue these last couple of days. I guess I should have just asked you to come along in the first place, but I was so scared of what I might find."

"I totally understood, Lizzie, but when I heard the dread in your voice about going to see your mother in that home, I couldn't sit there in Charlotte any longer. It was my fault, and I couldn't stand to think of you anxious or sad because of me. The least I could do was to come and support you. Besides, I missed you."

Elizabeth knew he was trying to add some humor to his conversation, but she knew he meant it as well. "I missed you too, you know. I have gotten pretty used to having you around in an awfully short time. I will miss you when you go back to Detroit."

Dan had heard exactly what he was hoping to hear. He was hoping to keep this relationship going from now on, but he was going to take that one day at a time. For now, the important thing was getting home safely and then waiting for the trunk. With the trunk would come closure for both of them, he hoped.

"Did your brother ever get hold of you this week? I called him and let him know that I found your father and suggested he come to Charlotte next week. I hope that was okay with you. I felt after all the drama, we both owed him some explanations. You know, I think I woke him up twice in one evening."

Elizabeth laughed at that one. "That doesn't surprise me. He sleeps in his chair in the evenings and then goes to bed early. I think he must get up by five every morning. He finally got me after a couple days of phone tag. That was fine. I am very glad that he is coming. We don't see enough of each other, and this will just be one visit that wasn't a holiday. It will be nice to see him. Maybe all of this will cause us to make the effort to be in better contact with each other."

The drive home was peaceful and relaxing. Elizabeth was very happy that Dan had flown out so he could help her drive back. It had been a successful trip but a terribly wearing trip emotionally. Elizabeth felt peaceful. She had done all she could do; so she got comfortable, put her head back, and was fast asleep by the time they were just a few miles down the road.

Dan looked over at her asleep beside him. It was like seeing her that day on the plane for the first time. Twenty years of looking for someone who could take Emily's place, and here she was, sitting right beside him. Whatever was in the trunk, he had already found what he had been waiting for all these years.

CHAPTER 11

The Trunk: Elizabeth
Discovers the Truth

The trunk arrived just as Elizabeth had expected, only two weeks after she left Mayfield. It was just enough time to get settled down before any more trauma could happen. Her brother had come for his visit, and she and Dan had finally managed to fill him in on every single detail. It took some doing, but they managed to get the whole story told. Peter spent most of his visit shaking his head over the whole thing.

"If I had not been a witness to all this, I would have never believed it. I doubt I will ever tell the story to anyone either because no one would believe me."

Elizabeth thought he might have been right. It was all so strange that she wasn't sure she even believed it, and certainly she would never understand.

Rachel had gotten the barn pictures to the printers, and the calendars were waiting for her when she returned. She was very pleased with them. She had not really expected they would come out as well as they did. She hoped everyone she had on her list to receive a copy and would be as pleased with them as she was.

She had declined any more book signing tours. Enough was enough for Elizabeth. She was ready to just stay home and once again enjoy the life of retirement, especially since she had someone to enjoy it with now. Dan was a constant companion, and while it was more company than she had known in several years, she enjoyed it very much. He seemed to be spending less and less time in Detroit and more and more time in Charlotte.

There was only one more bridge to cross, and it had just arrived. The trunk arrived late in the afternoon. The deliverymen had been kind enough to carry it in and set it in her living room. She had left it alone to finish some work and eat supper. Now, she sat on the floor of her living room and waited for courage to open the trunk. She was sure that somewhere in here would be all the answers to what had happened to her. There certainly was no logical answer, so there had to be some illogical explanation; and if it wasn't within this chest, then it was nowhere.

Her sister had sent along a note, addressed to her and attached to the top of the trunk.

Dear Elizabeth,

    I have looked into the trunk, and I realized there is nothing in here that really concerns me. I have left it intact as I found it. There are some journals in the bottom, which I am sure will probably solve your mysteries for you. I did not read them or even unwrap all of Aunt Emily's treasures. I left that for you. I hope this beautiful little chest holds all the treasures that you and Dan have been looking for.

    When it is all over, I hope that you will give me a call and fill me in on the final outcome. I believe I have finally adjusted to the idea that I have a sister, and I even think it is a good idea. Mother continues the same. There were a few times since you were here that she asked me if I had seen Aunt Emily, but she doesn't seem to be upset by the idea. Please keep in touch. I am looking forward to hear from you.

Your newfound sister,

Paula Sue

The trunk was not as large as Elizabeth had imagined it would be. It probably was two and a half feet wide and four feet long. It was as deep as it was wide. The lid was curved with metal pieces alternating with wood. The metal had been tooled and painted with flowers and leaves. One handle was broken, but otherwise the little trunk was in very nice condition. The latches and lock were still in working order. She pictured in her mind a young woman packing her most precious belongings away in this beautiful trunk much as she had packed away her own family memories in a storage box. She thought how generations come and go, but we don't really change all that much. We all feel the need to leave some legacy for the next generation in the form of family mementos and pictures.

Slowly she turned the little key in the latch. It opened easily. She lifted the lid. The very first thing in the trunk was a beautiful old doll with blonde curls. The dress had yellowed with age, but the doll itself was in excellent condition. Elizabeth could see a young girl on Christmas morning when she found this treasure under the tree. How special that must have been. The trunk opened up a world of excitement. It was full of small treasures, but the most important ones were what appeared to be journals packed in the very bottom. She pulled them out from under all the other contents.

Elizabeth opened the top one. The first page was the date.

May 5, 1905
My Journal by Emily

She unpacked the rest of the journals. There were six of them in all. They started in 1903, and the last entry appeared to be in 1905. Elizabeth had no verbal description for the feeling that had developed in her stomach and that was moving up into her throat.

This woman, her great aunt, had lived and died exactly when she had written that Dan had lived. The term "creepy" didn't start to describe what she was feeling now.

She didn't want to do this alone. She closed the trunk, went to the kitchen, and made a pot of coffee. Next, she picked up the phone and dialed the number she had found herself dialing a lot these days.

"Dan?"

"Hey, I was just thinking about you."

"Good thoughts I hope. I just received a package late this afternoon."

"Was it the trunk?"

"Yes, and I was hoping that you weren't too busy. I don't think I have the courage to do this alone."

"Is the coffee on?"

Elizabeth laughed. "Gallons of it."

"Okay, I am on my way. Have you eaten?"

"No, I was so anxious to get started with the trunk. I never thought of it."

"I'll bring something. Give me about an hour."

"I will wait for you. I think there are some things in there you should be here to see."

Elizabeth went back to the living room to further investigate the contents of the trunk, but the journals were not something she wanted to read without Dan. There were small glass figurines that had been carefully wrapped, a little silver link purse with a chain handle, a white fan covered in white feathers, and several pairs of eyeglasses. Each item had been carefully wrapped and tucked into a spot as if the owner of the trunk was preserving it all for some future generations.

There were some old books of assorted shapes and sizes. Poetry and novels carefully wrapped and saved for another day. One book caught her eye. It was leather bound, and when she picked it up, the leather rubbed off on her hands, but the pages seemed to be almost alive and were still in a very good condition. The title page caught her off guard—*The Union of Souls Across the Ages*. A strange sensation came over Elizabeth as though this little book held the key to the whole mystery. She would read it in its entirety later, but she took some time to glance through it. It was just as she had described the little book in her story. Not only did it contain stories of other time travels, but it gave what amounted to meditation instructions. They were meant to enable one to leave their time and place and transport themselves elsewhere. She wondered if Emily had studied and studied this. Perhaps that is how she was able to communicate with Elizabeth. She set the book aside and continued with the rest of the contents.

There was a picture of a young woman with dark hair and eyes. She seemed to have great determination on her face, and even in the brown photograph, her eyes were incredibly expressive. She was wearing a white dress and carrying a broad-brimmed white hat. Looking at it, Elizabeth realized why Dan had stared at her so hard on the plane. She looked amazingly like her great aunt Emily. It must have made Dan feel like he was seeing a ghost to see her sitting there next to his seat on the plane.

Under the journals were stacks of loose papers on which Emily had done sketches. There were lovely barns, several of the meadow, and others of farm animals. The very last drawing lay on the bottom of the trunk facedown. Elizabeth saw her hand shaking as she started to turn over the paper. From the back side, she knew it was the sketch of a face, and she was sure whose face it would be. Still it took her breath away when she finally lifted it from the trunk and looked at it. There in her hands was a face of a man, a man she now knew, but a man she had once drawn herself from who knew where. He was twenty years younger and very handsome; but still, even then, he had that deep frown on his face. Gazing at it, she began to realize how deep her feelings were for Dan.

The doorbell rang. She jerked so hard she pulled a leg muscle. She must have been in a trance or something; she didn't know how long she had been sitting there staring at that drawing.

"Dan! Oh, Dan, boy, do I need you here."

The frown on his face deepened. "Is it bad news? Was the trunk empty?"

"No, far from it. Maybe we should eat first. You are going to need all the strength you can get. There is nothing in there that can't wait till after dinner. I'm starving."

Elizabeth had not realized how much she grown accustomed to Dan in the last few months. She was so very comfortable with him and enjoyed his company. She missed him when he was away. She liked having him across the table from her even if she did still believe it was really Emily he loved. She would accept that if she could have him around more.

Dan was looking at Elizabeth, thinking to himself how much he had grown to care for her in the last few months. Although she looked much like Emily and had many of her qualities, she was her own person; and he had grown very fond of the person she was. He didn't know how she was feeling about him because they had never really discussed their relationship. They had been so involved in the hunt for answers, they had missed the most important thing—the two of them. When the time was right, he must discuss that with her.

They ate hurriedly. Neither of them wanted to spend more time away from the thing they had both been waiting to investigate. They moved back into the living room and sat in front of the trunk. "Well, we have put it off as long as we can. I guess we should face the contents of the trunk and see if the hunt was worth all the effort."

Dan looked through all of the things that Elizabeth had unwrapped. She showed him the brown book, which she had set aside to read later. Most of the items were of little interest to him. He had never seen any of them. Emily had never brought anything to the meadow with her.

They found drawing pencils, delicate handkerchiefs, a pair of spats, some very old school readers, and more assorted personal items. Elizabeth wondered if Emily had packed this when she knew she was dying or if someone packed up her things after she died. She was guessing Emily did this, for each item seemed to have been tenderly packed away as only their owner would want to do.

Elizabeth showed Dan the barn sketches that Emily had done. "Apparently, I came by my love of barns quite naturally."

"I see that."

"This is probably why I felt so very attached to the barn near your meadow," Elizabeth said as she showed him several pictures of that same barn she was so fond of. The pictures were different. Emily's barn was new, with haystacks and animals, and had children playing in and around it. It was alive.

"Did you know that she drew this?" Elizabeth held up the picture that had held her spellbound. It was Dan. The likeness between the drawing she had done for her book and the drawing that Emily had done was astounding.

"No, I knew she liked to draw, but I never really saw any of her work. She had to have done that from memory because she never brought her drawing to the meadow. I think she made me much better looking than I really was." He laid the sketches carefully back in the bottom of the trunk.

"I have been wondering a lot since we came home if this was really worth doing. It was dreadful and draining emotionally on you, and that made it hard on me as well. At least, Lizzie, it gained you a new sister, and it has given me someone that I have grown very fond of."

"You only feel that because you see Emily in me." There, she had said it at last. She had never had the courage to say that before; but with the end of the search now on her living room floor, she did not feel restrained to speak her mind.

"No, Lizzie, I see Emily in you all right, but I see someone completely different as well. Someone I have come to know and grown to love. I am hoping you have some of those same feelings for me."

Elizabeth sat still beside him for a moment; then she turned to face him. She wrapped her arms around his neck and hung on tightly. His arms encircled her waist and returned the hold. "I could never have done this without you, and now I can't imagine being without you. I hate it when you leave for Detroit. I feel so alone now when you are gone."

He was still holding tight, feeling his world had come full circle, when she loosened her hold and moved away.

"Why don't we finish what we started here, and then we can move on with our relationship." They had saved the journals for last, and it was going to be the hardest. Hopefully they would tell Dan everything he wanted to know about Emily and what happened to her.

Before leaving the trunk and its contents, they packed away each item as carefully as Emily had put them in there. Elizabeth had felt no emotional connection with either her mother or her sister; but she felt as though she had known Emily, and she wanted to save her things. Not much in the contents gave up any special secrets. It had all been normally personal and home possessions. Their last hope lay in the books, those journals Emily had so carefully packed away in the bottom of her trunk.

CHAPTER 12

The Journals

Having looked through the entire contents of the trunk, they replaced everything carefully except the journals. Those they took to the couch and curled up together to do some deep studying.

They started with the first one. Dan read the journal aloud, and Elizabeth listened intently.

May 3, 1903

I am writing these journals for you, Mama, so that you will know how much I love you and Papa and how much I appreciated everything you both have done for me. I know it has been harder on you than it has on me. After all, I am only dying; you must watch me do so and live on afterward. I know that must be hard. Please take heart and know that I am at peace and will be safe and happy on the other side.

"Did you know that she was dying?"

"No, I had no idea until the week just before she stopped coming to the meadow. I knew she didn't look well, but she always seemed so happy."

"Did you know why she stopped coming?"

"I didn't know for sure, but I had a good idea. After she didn't come for four or five days in a row, I was sure she would never come again. I don't know how I knew, but I just knew. I was sure she must have died. Otherwise, she would have never left me. I was sure of that."

Elizabeth's husband had died ten years earlier after a long battle with cancer. They had enjoyed a wonderful life together and a hard struggle to the end. Now she tired to imagine how she would feel if this had been a journal written by him, which she had only just now found. She moved closer to Dan wishing she could take away his frown and sadness.

They read on. The journal was beautifully written, and there were entries for almost every day. Emily had just made a short note each day. Some of them were about something that had happened; some were just thoughts she had. Still others were expressions of feelings that came to her. They revealed a kind and tender person, whose positive attitude toward life and death seemed to give her great strength.

> *May 30, 1903*
> *I don't fear dying. Everyone must take that path at one moment or another. What I fear the most is dying without completion. I suppose many have died not knowing what true love really is, but my heart's desire would have been to discover that for myself before I left this place. I am discounting the girlhood crushes, and am referring to the deeply binding relationship that only mature people can feel for one another.*

They looked through the entire first journal, not reading every entry but watching the dates on the pages. They could go back later and read the whole journal. There were entries of encouragement to her family, of love for life and the earth, and philosophical ideas she had felt concerning her approaching death. There were even small-scattered sketches of some of the things she talked about seeing.

> *August 10, 1904*
> *I love to draw. The old barn near the meadow is my favorite art object. I have drawn it from*

every angle. Its character and durability give me courage and strength. There are other barns on the farm as well. All of them have found their way to my journal several times.

One of the things I miss the most is romping in the barn. My goodness, I loved that barn as a child. Still, when I am in the meadow, I have the dreadful urge to climb the loft and swing out on a rope to the ground below as we used to do when we were children. I suppose the wonderful barn will stand forever. Papa and the neighbors built it in just a day.

September 24, 1904

I am glad for the years I was able to teach. I always loved children. My students and their achievements gave meaning to my life. My parents have been wonderfully supportive. I know this has been hard on Mama. She always has such a sad look in her eyes when she watches me. I wish she wouldn't be sad. I'm not.

December 16, 1904

Sarah was here today with her children. She seems happy enough. At least she is busy. The boys are growing like young saplings, and the *girls are beginning to blossom. Evelyn is the one I worry about. She is so quiet and withdrawn. She seems to have inherited my artistic ability for she usually finds some quiet place and amuses herself by drawing. Still, I worry about her for she doesn't seem to have the ability to communicate well other than with her drawings.*

Many of the details in the journals were clues to the family that Elizabeth had been searching for. Siblings, cousins, aunts, uncles—all listed, named, and discussed in these journals. Her sister would never know what a gift she had given Elizabeth or how much it would reveal to her. This Evelyn, who was Emily's shy niece, was none other than Elizabeth's own mother.

Through these books, Elizabeth found an extended family that she had never known. She had no desire to find them, but their personalities were of interest to her. Characteristics she had that neither of her adoptive parents possessed now belonged to her by birth. There had been many times down through the years when Elizabeth had wondered about her heritage. She wondered which one of her parents were artistic, compulsive, stubborn, and all the other personality traits that she was. When she saw some of her own traits in her daughter, it made her wonder even that much more. Now she had great insight into her own personality framework.

December 18, 1904

Uncle Raymond was here today. He brought me some more drawing materials from town. I know that he encourages me to draw because he loves to do so himself. Since Mama never draws, I guess I took my talent after him. Often he tried to show me little tricks to make my barns look more and more realistic.

They skimmed three of the journals with nothing of any serious interest in them. The last journal appeared to be dated 1905. That was the summer Emily had met Dan in the meadow, and that was the summer she died. It was getting late, and Elizabeth was worried about Dan. He seemed to be happy to have found the journals, but now she wondered if she should have read through them first before she showed them to him.

"Let's take a break and have a snack or something. My back is tired, and my stomach is growling."

Dan seemed annoyed at the interruption, but he glanced at his watch and agreed. "I am sorry, Lizzie. I had no idea it had gotten so late. I know you have been exhausted. It is almost midnight. Would you like to finish this another time?"

"I am tired. Do you really want to wait till later to read these?"

"No, I am sure I would not sleep a wink all night, but I can leave and come back tomorrow. I don't want to make this harder on you than it already has been."

"Let's just take a quick break and start again. I don't think I would sleep either, knowing you were home waiting to read the last journal, and I don't want you to read it alone either. How about some ice cream? Strawberry or cookie dough?"

Dan stood and stretched. Lizzie had been right. They had been sitting a very long time. His mind was wide-awake, but his body definitely needed to move around. "Strawberry please."

Elizabeth felt uneasy about continuing on with the journals. She was sure from this point on they would involve Dan, and she was not sure how he would react to them. Still, that had to be his choice. She knew Emily would have meant him to read them if she could have given them to him herself. Now she was just doing it for her. The stretch was good. Her body had grown stiff sitting in one position so long, and the ice cream was a welcome break.

"Okay, let's get back to work here. How about if I read for a while and you listen?" Elizabeth took up the last journal and started on the very first page.

May 5, 1905

Papa left the meadow untouched just for me. He knows how I love to wander through it and sit by the brook watching the water flow by. It is the one place my body and mind find rest. Well hidden from the world, I can walk there in my nightgown and with my bare feet. Mama always makes me wear a big brim hat to keep off the sun's ray, but

I take it off as soon as I get to the meadow. The sun feels wonderful on my face.

Elizabeth stopped reading. "I wonder what she would think if she knew her beloved meadow was still exactly the same a hundred years later." She hadn't expected Dan to answer for she was talking more to herself than to him.

"I am sure she would not be surprised." His voice cut through her thoughts.

"No, I supposed she wouldn't. She would probably even have expected that." Elizabeth refocused on the journal.

I have met so few men in my life that intrigued me. This one certainly did. Perhaps the most intriguing thing about him was that he was in the meadow at all. No one ever comes to the meadow. That is why I am so comfortable there. I wasn't sure what to do. He looked so different from any of the men I am used to seeing as well. I can't imagine where he came from or how he found his way to our meadow. There he was, just sitting by the brook, looking at it as though he might find some of life's answers floating by. Handsome, definitely, and close to my age I suspect. Oh, I do hope he comes back again sometime. Next time I will not be frightened of him. I will speak to him when he speaks to me. This time I just ran away.

"This was just as you described it, Dan. It is still beyond comprehension how this could really have taken place, but here we have true written record. By now, we already knew the truth, but it is nice to see it in writing. I guess it keeps me from thinking I am completely crazy." Dan didn't reply. He seemed lost in thought somewhere, so Elizabeth read on.

Wednesday

That strange man was in our meadow again today walking around. He spoke to me. "Hello," he said, "who are you, and where did you come from?" Who was he to be asking me who I was? Who was he, and why had he come back again in our meadow? Of course, I answered him, "I'm Emily, Emily Stamps. I come from the home just over the hill. This is our meadow." He had a very strange look on his face when I said that. Apparently he thought he owned the meadow. He mistakenly thought he had bought a huge farm in these parts that included the meadow and the brook. I must talk to Father about it tonight when he gets home. I set him straight in no uncertain terms that he didn't own our meadow and never would. He left without arguing with me.

The encounters with Dan each had a short sentence or two about them. Elizabeth began to wish she had been able to read the journals before she wrote her book. Perhaps she could have done them justice. The meeting, the building of a relationship, and the love that developed was all much better described by Emily. She was becoming just a little uncomfortable reading these private thoughts and accounts of Emily's love. For Dan, it was beautiful memories; but for Elizabeth, it seemed to be a rude intrusion on her part.

"Would you like to just take this home with you and finish it there? I don't want to intrude on your private life."

"Of course I don't, Lizzie. Besides, I don't think I could bear to read them alone. Please stay with me thorough this. I want you to be here."

The saga continued. Emily described their meeting and the growth of their love.

Oh my, I hope he comes back again. I feel myself getting excited just thinking about the stranger in the meadow. How hopeless it is for me to even want to see him. My future at best is bleak and short. All I have are a few fleeting months. What could I ever offer him?

He was there again this afternoon. My, he is so very serious looking. You would think a smile would be easier to wear than that deep frown. Maybe he frowns because, like me, his life has been shortened. It is not really anything to frown about. I have enjoyed every day I have lived, and I am not afraid to die.

The writing of thoughts and sharing of secrets were written beautifully in these books. Just reading them was an incredible experience.

"I guess you have always had that frown."

Dan smiled. "Yes, I guess I have. I never really notice."

"I thought maybe it had come with age and wisdom." Elizabeth smiled but then continued reading. It was growing very late, and she was exhausted. The emotional strain of reliving Dan's deep love for someone else was beginning to take its toll.

I told Sarah about the stranger in the meadow. She didn't think it was a good idea to tell anyone else. Mama might not want me down there again if she thought there was some man there, and she would be even more concerned if she thought I was seeing visions. I'm sure Sarah is right. He will just be our secret.

Dan, his name is Dan Kerr. He has a very soft, deep voice with a very interesting accent. Apparently he is from somewhere in the North. Pity. The South is such a pleasant place. Maybe that is why he wanted to buy the farm. I forgot to ask him again about that.

Then, there it was, Dan's name—his entire name. If ever Elizabeth had doubted this story, and she had not, all of that would have been erased by the one swipe of Emily's pen that spelled out the letters, *Dan Kerr*.

It is a mystery to me how he walks and talks with me. Apparently this man whom I have fallen deeply in love with is not within my lifetime. I suppose I must concede that he has bought the farm but at a later date. My fervent prayer is that he will preserve the meadow at all cost. It gives me such peace when my soul is troubled.

He held me today in his arms as we sat by the brook. What a grand feeling. I have had such a limited life that this type of relationship was never afforded to me. Now in my twilight days, I find such glorious love around me, I sometimes can hardly breathe.

He has such a frown on his face that sometimes I want to laugh at him. I always find life so pleasant and happy, even in pain, that I think it would be hard to frown so much. It gives him a worried look. When he smiles, it makes my whole day bright.

Elizabeth finally laughed out loud. "She has talked about your frown on several occasions. Did you ever smile?"

With that, Dan did smile. "I guess I don't smile often, do I? Back then, I spent a lot of the time that I was with her trying to figure out how such a thing could be happening. It was very unusual to find someone on my property who had come from a hundred years in my past. Now I only wish I had relaxed more, smiled more, and just enjoyed the moment. I had no way of knowing then it would end so suddenly."

"Isn't all life that way, Dan? One day we have someone or something; the next day it is gone. If we don't enjoy the moment, it passes unnoticed."

"Yes, now that you say it like that, I guess it is."

Sometimes the confines of his arms would seem to be all I need to sustain life. I feel so wonderful and so healthy and so alive when I am with him. I can't start to understand how this has happened, but it has made my life complete.

Wednesday

I believe there is nothing we can hope for more in our life than deep and trusting love. I always loved my students and my siblings and my parents, but all those pale with the love I feel for Dan. I don't know how long we can continue to find each other here in this meadow, but someday I know we will find each other beyond the meadow. That is the day I long for. That is the day I will strive for.

Elizabeth stopped and looked at Dan. He was motionless. She wondered if he was even hearing the words she was reading. Perhaps he had moved past the journals and was walking again in the meadow with Emily. He stirred. "It's okay, Lizzie, we are almost finished here."

CHAPTER 13

Closure for Dan

Elizabeth and Dan read the journals until the early hours of the morning. Emily had kept a careful but brief record of her life for several years. It had been a long process and a lot of reading. The last few entries were the hardest to read. By now, Dan was so overcome with emotion that Elizabeth was unsure about trying to continue.

I have no secrets to Dan, except the biggest secret of all. I can't tell him that my heart is failing. We are so happy that I couldn't bear to interject any sad thought into what little time we have together. I never minded leaving this earth before, but now I feel I shall miss Dan terribly. I wonder if we are able to reconnect with the one we love from the other side. If I am allowed to be a guardian angel, I want to be his.

"Are you going to be okay to finish this? We can just wait until another time, or I can just send them home with you. Maybe you would rather finish them alone." She was genuinely concerned for him, and she felt as though she was an intruder in a private meeting.

Dan had been sitting there listening and watching Elizabeth read. The light was reflecting off her hair showing the flecks of gray that were beginning to overtake the black, but even with those, she looked so much like Emily it was almost ghostly. There she sat looking like an older version of the young woman he had loved and lost years ago, reading from her very private diary as though it were her own.

96

"No, I find it very pleasant to hear you read Emily's words and see you as you read it. I suppose I am hearing nothing I didn't really know or at least suspect. It is just hearing you read what Emily is saying and seeing you sitting there looking so very much like her. Really, Lizzie, it is almost like having Emily here with me."

"I'm sorry, Dan. I know this has to open up old wounds that probably should have been left to heal. I guess we both made a choice to look backward. There was a price to pay for that."

"It was my choice. I was the one pushing for this. No, I am very happy to see and read the journals. What precious things they are. What wonderful insight they give me to someone I loved so very much and lost so long ago. I will always be grateful to you for sharing them with me."

"They aren't really mine, Dan. They belong to you."

"Sad as they make me, at least they assure me that Emily was as much in love with me as I was with her. She became such an integral part of my life that I was never able to imagine life with anyone else."

Elizabeth said nothing but turned back to the journal and continued reading. For her, there had been little or no emotion involved. It was merely an interesting story full of names, places, and facts from her past. For Dan, it was another story. She had watched him as they went through the journals, and it was obvious how very hard this was on him. It was hard on her as well because she loved Dan very much, and these journals reconnected him with the woman he had loved and lost. She was feeling as though Dan was slipping back through time, to another place, and to someone else's arms. This last journal was becoming emotional, even for her, but she could see the end in sight; and by now she was ready to finish this whole ordeal.

Well, Mama, I guess it is okay to tell you this now, for when you read this I will be gone. I have found a wonderful man. I have fallen deeply in love, and I feel that finally my life has found completion. The deepest desire I had for my life before I died has been fulfilled. He is no one that you or Papa would be familiar with. He has come to my meadow from another time and place. Apparently he has purchased the farm and intends to build houses on it. No need to worry, it is not in your day or mine. Somehow, either the meadow or I have projected into the future, or he has come backward in time to us. Either way, these last few months have been the most wonderful months I could ever imagine experiencing. I just wanted to let you know how very happy they have been.

The last entry in the book was addressed directly to Dan as though Emily had known in her heart that someday he would find them and be able to read what had been in her heart. Elizabeth believed that Emily was convinced that she would somehow get these journals to Dan, and he would know, without a doubt, what he had meant to her.

Dear Dan,

I wish that you, as well as my parents, could be reading this journal, for it would give you some peace as well to know that I am leaving this world with such love in my heart, and you are responsible for that. You will move on with your life, and I hope you will think back of me fondly. Please remember that if ever you think of me, it could mean you are reaching across time; so enjoy, my love.

At this point, Elizabeth was almost as overcome with emotion as Dan. She paused. "Oh, Dan, If only you could have read her journals years ago. It would have given you such comfort over the years. You would have known what happened to her, and you would have known how fulfilling you made her life."

"Yes, but I think I already knew how much it meant to her because whatever it was for Emily, it was that much and more for me. It would have been easier if she would have only told me she was dying; maybe I could have done something for her."

"That would have put another element into your relationship, one of sadness. Besides, that might have been risky. Altering events from the past can change a multitude of things. Perhaps it was best that life played itself out as it was supposed to have done. You had a purpose and a place in time as did Emily. It was the same place; it just happened to be in a different time. You were there in her time for her when she needed someone most. You gave her love and showed her how wonderful life can be when it is devoted to someone else. That was the greatest gift you could ever give anyone. It was the completion to her life she was searching for. Maybe, somehow that is what enabled her to reach across time and space. It was the one thing she wanted more than anything else—to love deeply and be loved. It is too bad you were left with such emptiness after she was gone. You might have not felt that had you known you had fulfilled her greatest desire." Elizabeth continued to read.

I am not able to go to the meadow anymore. My body just doesn't have the strength. I'm afraid my bed is now my confine. Dan, you will never know what happened to me; but, my love, I promise you this—I will find you again. I am not sure how or when, but I am sure that we will be together once more. I promise. No love, as strong as ours, can be destroyed by death or time. If you do not wait for me, I will be sad, but I will understand, my love. You have no way of knowing that I will always be trying to find you somehow.

Somewhere out there will be that perfect someone, someone who will reach out to you for me. My hope is when they do, you recognize what is happening. Reach back to them, my darling. Know that I have had a hand in the union and embrace it as you would embrace me.

I only wish I could tell you how wonderful you made my last months here. I never imagined I would find such happiness. We are never more blessed than when we are totally loved by another and are able to return that devotion.

God be with you, my love.

Emily

Elizabeth closed the last journal. They had all been read. What a tender and loving soul her aunt Emily had been. She could understand how Dan would have fallen very deeply in love with her. She slowly stacked the journals together and retied them with the ribbon that had held them captive. She handed them to Dan.

"These belong to you."

Dan looked at her in disbelief. "They are yours, Lizzie; she was your aunt. I cannot take these."

"I could not possibly keep your treasure. I am sure Emily would have wanted you to have these. I am sure she may have written the last one just for you."

Dan took the books. He held them close as though he was holding Emily once more. He said nothing. Elizabeth realized he was in such an emotional state that conversation was almost not possible.

"Would you like another cup of coffee?" She was sure he didn't, but there was nothing left to say at the moment.

"Thanks, but I think I will just head home. It is so very late, or is it early now? I cannot begin to tell you how much I appreciate everything you have done, Lizzie. I would never have imagined it would all end here in a trunk of personal effects."

"No, but wasn't it wonderful of her to leave behind the answers to both our questions?"

"Yes, when we started this search, I never expected such success. It is all thanks to you and your willingness to help me. I can only hope it was not detrimental to you. I can never repay you."

"You owe me nothing, Dan, and I am fine. I needed answers myself."

"Well, I think I will get going, Lizzie. I'll call you tomorrow."

"Okay, good night."

Elizabeth closed the door behind him. She didn't know how she had expected this all to end, but this was not the ending she had hoped for. She had wanted him to put down the journals and profess his undying love for her and her alone. She had wanted to hear his tell her that Emily was a past ghost and would always be nothing more now that he had found her. She had to hope that when Dan recovered he would do exactly what he had just said he would do. He would call tomorrow.

They both needed some time alone now. They both had some sorting to do. Somehow the past and the present and the future had gotten entangled, and it would take some thought to untangle them.

CHAPTER 14

The Final Chapter

Well, that was that. The trunk had been inspected, the journals read, and Dan was gone. It was almost morning once more. Elizabeth tried to remember how many times in the last several months she had experienced these sleepless nights and watched the sun come up from her kitchen table over a cup of coffee. The difference was she was lonesome now, and instead of a search to look forward to, she was left with only a few ends to tie up and an empty place in her heart that hadn't been there before.

There, in one large manila envelope, was her entire past—a past apart from the past she was familiar with but hers nonetheless. She had put all the information she had gathered, all the papers and legal documents and any other notes she had made in one envelope. There were the pictures she had copied from the yearbook and even the maps the desk clerk had been so kind to draw for her. She could hold it in her hand. She could open it up. She could drop it in the trash can. Maybe she should have never gone looking for her past because she wasn't good at dealing with anything but the here and now. How could she now deal with what should be done or what could have been done or what should be left alone? She emptied the contents onto the table for one last look.

She picked up the picture of her mother's graduation class and studied it for what she promised to be the last time. There they were, her mother and her mother. It still seemed so very strange to see the two of them standing in the same place at the same time. Her adoptive mother—young, hopeful, only sixteen years old—graduating with another young woman who would have an impact on her life that she never expected. Standing on the back row was her biological mother. The young woman who would fall in love, have a baby, pass it on to one of her classmates, and then go on with her life as though nothing had happened. They both looked so young, so full of hope, and so ready for whatever the future would bring. How could they possibly have known?

Elizabeth knew she owed them both a lot. She owed her biological mother her life, both physically and emotionally. She had given birth to her, she had given her the physical characteristics and personality that had molded her life, and then she had given her the greatest opportunity of all. She had given her a new chance for life with two people who wanted a baby girl more than anything in the world and who loved her unconditionally and totally until their dying breath. What greater gift could she have given her infant daughter? Elizabeth had always just assumed her mother birthed her then left her. Now, she realized her mother had made arrangements for her best friend to rear her baby. She was sure that had to have made it easier to move on with her own life, knowing that someone she loved and trusted was guiding the life of her own flesh and blood. While she could not imagine giving up her own daughter and never knowing or seeing her, she was not feeling judgmental in any way. She had been born in a different time and place.

She owed her adoptive mother her very being. It was she who was there through every childhood illness, every nightmare, and every wonderful event. It was she who had made personal sacrifices to give her daughter all the advantages imaginable. It was that wonderful mother who had made the most adoring grandmother for her daughter anyone could ever have imagined. They had been such wonderful friends. Elizabeth felt a deep love for them both. She tried to imagine how her mother must have felt when her best friend Mary called and told her that not only was she going to receive a baby, but it was going to be the offspring of her best friend. It was still a lot to deal with. She wondered if her mother had reservations about taking the baby of her best friend or if she preferred to know the parents of her child.

She put the picture back in its envelope. As she did, a small slip of paper dropped from the envelope. It was the name of her father and his phone number that Dan had given her. She had never called that number. She turned the paper over and over in her hands. No, she didn't feel the need to call this person. There was nothing really about him that made him her father except his relationship with a woman whom he probably hardly knew. They had been thrown together in a time of great emotional struggle. They had turned to each other for comfort. He probably never expected to return home alive. Mary had explained to her how her mother tried and tried to reach him after she discovered she was pregnant; but he had left for duty, and she had no other recourse but home. So he had never known he had a daughter, and there was no need to tell him now.

She saw no need to contact this man now. She had been given a real father. One who read to her at bedtime, played with her, taught her how to garden, and always took time from his work to hear any problems. No, she didn't think anyone could ever take his place. She had adored him. She walked with him and talked with him until she was sure she must have worn him out. He always seemed happy to see her coming. There was absolutely no reason to contact this stranger, especially not at this time in her life. Many times, it is better to just let things be. It would serve no useful purpose to call this man and announce that he had fathered a child sixty-two years ago. She slid the paper back into the envelope from whence it came.

She took the envelope to the living room and knelt by the old trunk. She studied the tooling work on the metal parts. What a treasure, the trunk itself had been to someone in its day. She could just picture her great aunt Emily packing her few possessions away carefully for someone in her future. Maybe as she wrapped each item she smiled, thinking of someone in later years unwrapping them with gleeful surprise. She had enjoyed opening each special trinket, and now she respectfully returned them to their original place. When all of the items had been rewrapped and packed carefully away, Elizabeth put the envelope with her birth certificate and all the pictures and notes from the search on the very top. The closing of the lid seemed cold and final, almost like the shutting of a casket lid but with one difference. Someday her daughter would find the trunk as Paula Sue had, and it would be a pleasure to look through all the memories from the past.

It was finished. The trunk was emptied and repacked. The journals had been read. Elizabeth had found her roots, and Dan had found Emily. Elizabeth could not be sure what had really happened, but she had her theories. The only key to the explanation had to be in her ability to meditate. By making her mind empty and open, she had allowed Emily to communicate with her. It wasn't the move to North Carolina as Elizabeth had originally thought; it was the timing. Emily knew which year to find Dan and that had been the year Elizabeth had written the book. It all made perfect sense. Or did it? It still seemed like something from the twilight zone. Either way, it was finished. Everyone had their closure. Or did they?

Elizabeth was wishing she had never met Dan. She was unhappy about finding her birth parents. She wasn't unhappy about finding the rest of her roots. Losing Dan was what was making her unhappy. She had grown very fond of him. Okay, more than that—she was very deeply in love with Dan. They had known each other in such a short time, but Elizabeth felt as though it had been forever. Now that he had his answers and was gone, she would miss him very much. Even though he said he was not going away when this was over, when he walked out that door with the journals, she felt as though it was the last time she would see him. She folded her arms, laid her head on the trunk, and did something she had not done in since that day in Mayfield. She sobbed.

Now, not only did she feel very sad, but she was feeling very foolish. She was sitting on her living room floor at four o'clock in the morning, sobbing. It felt good. It had been a long tense couple of months, and now she guessed it was okay to express her sadness and relieve all that tension. Besides, no one would ever know but her.

Her phone rang. Who on earth would be calling at four in the morning? A quick look at her caller ID told her it was Dan. She composed herself and answered the phone.

"Hello, Dan."

"Did I wake you? You sound sleepy."

"No," she lied, not wanting him to think she was just sitting in the middle of the floor weeping. "I was just having a final cup of coffee. I wasn't feeling very sleepy."

"Me either. Do you have enough for me?"

Elizabeth was thrilled, but she didn't want to sound over anxious; and she was wondering why he would want to return to her house at four in the morning, but she didn't care. "Sure, I will put another pot on. It should be ready by the time you get here."

"I doubt that. I'm standing at your front door."

Elizabeth opened the door. He was right. There he was. He took one look at her and realized immediately she had been crying. Her eyes were red and swollen, and she had that look of devastation. He reached for her with both arms. "You weren't sleepy, were you? You have been crying. Did I do this to you?"

"No, really, it is okay. I did it to myself."

"What do you mean?"

"I let myself fall deeply in love with someone who was just as deeply in love with a ghost. What could I expect? Closure for you meant sadness for me, but I am happy for you."

"That isn't true, Lizzie. I loved Emily some twenty years ago and never found anyone who could take her place, that is, until I met you. It isn't the ghost of Emily that I am in love with. It is you. I started home, but I realized how foolish I had been to leave you sitting here alone. By doing so, I gave you a chance to doubt me and us. I didn't want to go home alone either. I just didn't know how you felt, and it was very late; and I guess I needed a few minutes to clear my head. The journals were an emotional trip for me."

"I can't even imagine how you must have been feeling."

"I don't know if I could even describe it either, but what I did realize was, I have the best of both worlds in you."

"What do you mean?"

"I mean, I have the amazing person you are and some inherited characteristics of Emily's. What more can any man ask for. You are quite similar to your great aunt, but you are definitely not her. I knew from the moment I stepped on that airplane and saw you there asleep in the seat that I loved you. If it is at all possible, I think I love you even more than I loved her."

"When you walked out the door with the journals, I felt as though you were walking away with another woman, and I would never see you again. I don't want you to ever leave again. I just can't imagine my life without you in it.

"I don't want to try to imagine my life without you, Lizzie. Are old people allowed to fall in love and marry?"

Elizabeth laughed. "Is that a proposal?"

"Definitely, but maybe we better iron out all the details later. Right now, maybe we better get some rest. Now that we have each other I believe we can sleep soundly."

"I am sure you are right."

Dan and Elizabeth made arrangements to have a small informal family wedding the following month. Nothing big, nothing really planned, just a few friends and family to help them launch their new life together. Elizabeth called Paula Sue and invited her and her family to come to Charlotte for the occasion. She suggested they stay with her so they would have some time to get to know one another. Paula graciously accepted.

There was one other very important guest at the wedding—Mary McCord. She was the key to Elizabeth's entire past. Not only had she shaped her future, but she had also helped her find her past. She had been a true friend her entire life to her high school buddies. Elizabeth considered her the best friend she had as well. Upon returning from Mayfield, she had kept in constant contact with Mary, reporting to her all the details involved in the final saga. She was thrilled to have her come to Charlotte, and it was even nicer that she and Paula Sue had come together. Life didn't get much better than this.

Peter came to Charlotte once again. That was more than the two of them had seen of each other in such a short time for years. "We must keep this going, Peter. I have missed having you to talk to."

"You are going to have someone to talk to all the time now, Lizzie, but we will try to stay in better contact. I promise."

The service was short; the reception was long. It gave everyone time to visit and relive the past few months. Surrounded by everyone she loved, Elizabeth could not have had better closure herself.

Rachel was thrilled to see her mom so happy, to meet an aunt she never knew she had, and, of course, as her mother had told her, it was all her fault.